INSIDE ALBERT SHIFTY

A Star Original

We found number 426 just where I'd said it'd be. Leaving Norman to guard the van, I hopped out, went up the concrete driveway and rang the bell. Chimes donged in the hall. I had a look round. Neat little garden, but no plastic gnomes in sight, thank God. I wiggled my fingers at Norman and he wiggled his back.

I heard the door behind me open. I turned . . .

By gum, she was a little cracker, blonde, nice face, dreamy eyes – and stacked. My eyes automatically dropped down her façade. Blimey, she was wearing shorts, *very* shorts, and sticking out of the bottoms were two of the shapeliest legs I'd drooled over in a long time. She was lovely.

Age? Oh . . . early twenties going on fifty-four sexually. She had a very naughty smile.

'Hi,' she beamed, working me over with the eyes which did a lightning fast trip up and down *my* façade before finally coming to rest in my eyes.

'Albert, I presume.'

I gave a little bow, knowing I was in friendly territory. 'Albert Shifty – at your undivided service . . .'

INSIDE ALBERT SHIFTY

Stanley Morgan

A STAR BOOK
published by
the Paperback Division of
W. H. ALLEN & Co. Ltd

A Star Book
Published in 1977
by the Paperback Division of
W. H. Allen & Co. Ltd
A Howard and Wyndham Company
123, King Street, London W6 9JG

Copyright © Stanley Morgan, 1977

Printed in Great Britain by
Hazell Watson & Viney Ltd, Aylesbury, Bucks.

ISBN 0 352 39623 7

CHAPTER ONE

BANG! . . . went my alarm clock.

No, on second thoughts THUD! would be a more accurate description of a boot striking a door, but let's not be pedantic about it.

'Yers?' I hollered.

'You awake, Albert?' enquired Norman's weedy squawk.

'No, mate. How about you?'

'It's ten past eight.'

'Thank you, my good man. What's the weather report?'

'Dry and sunny again, me tranny says. Temperature's in the mid-seventies.'

'Norman, old son, you have just made my day. Get cracking.'

As he clomped heavy-footed down the stairs to the bath-room, I skipped out of bed and headed for the window, threw back the curtains and blinded meself with sunlight. What a day! Up there, beyond the slate rooftops and grimy chimney pots of the tall Victorian monstrosities that run behind ours, the sky was as clear as a glass of water. The Met. boys had got it right for a change. It was going to be a scorcher.

Well, so much for the weather – but right then I had other things on my mind.

Opening my chest-of-drawers, I took out what I have always regarded to be one of my more worthwhile investments – a pair of Carl Zeiss Jenoptem 7 × 50 binoculars, a fantastic set of bins that cost me an Arab's ransom but which every morning paid for themselves eight times over in visual delight.

Now, I don't know about you, but the start of the day is very important to me. Get off to a lousy one and you never seem to catch up with yourself, somehow. Conversely, get it right in the first ten minutes and no matter what rubbish comes along to plague you later on, it can never really hurt you.

That being so, I always make a point of indulging in a few minutes' nature study as soon as I wake up. It sort of recharges the elemental batteries, if you know what I mean. Give me an eyeful of a seagull in graceful flight, a crow soaring high on a

5

Fulham thermal, or even a sparrow scratching its earhole, and I'm set up for the day. Sentimental, perhaps, but that's Albert Shifty for you.

So, easing back Mrs. Kranki's cement-coloured white net curtain, I got the bins to my eyes and picked up a blackbird taking a dust-bath in the roof gutter of number 76, the seedy, eight-million-roomed monument to bed-sit misery which lies directly behind our own eight-million-roomed ditto.

Ha ha, the cheeky little bugger was having a wonderful time, throwing into the air the dried-up accumulation of seventy years' gutter debris and letting it fall on his stupid head. Still, whatever turns you on. Live and let live is the Shifty motto. If the daft sod couldn't think of anything better to do than cover itself in gutter muck, who was I to criticise? Maybe *I* was missing a treat and didn't know it. Though if it was an early-morning dust-bath that turned me on, I'd have picked a more salubrious gutter than number 76 Canker Lane!

And that, I suppose, describes the Shifty philosophy in life as accurately as any other example. You've got to work it out for yourself, haven't you? Set your sights on what you want out of life and go after it your own way. Take no notice of what other people say, do it to suit yourself.

I swung the bins down on to a group of thrushes fighting over a crust in the manky back-garden of 76. Boy, they were going at it hammer-and-tongs, rising in a cloud of fluttering fury, pecking hell out of each other, making a terrible din. And now a big black crow joined them . . . no, he hadn't, he just whipped in while the thrushes were busy knocking seven bells out of one another and pinched the crust from under their very beaks.

See what I mean?

He'd worked it out for himself, played it solo, refused to join the rabble – and won the prize. Whoever it was who said 'Give me a committee and I'll give you chaos' certainly knew his onions. And that's the Shifty motto to a T.

That's why I work for myself.

Any job, big or small – from garden clearing to oven clean-ing, I'll have a go at anything.

'Let Albert Do It' my business card says. 'Painting, Decorat-

6

ing, Any Odd-job Around the Home. If you want a good job done – Let Albert Do It.'

My alarm clock, Norman, by the way, is my mate who lives in the next room to me, up here on the fifth floor of Mrs. Kranki's boarding house. He's a nice enough lad but gormless. It takes him five minutes to boil a three minute egg. But he's very willing, which is why I employ him. One of his jobs is to wake me every morning with a thump on the door because I can't stand being shattered awake by alarm bells.

Norman Norman his name is – and if I'd had parents like that I'd be missing a few slates, too. I'd also be missing a couple of parents!

Anyway, back to my nature study.

I swung the bins upwards from the garden of 76 and traversed six windows to the left, top floor, just in time to catch her drawing back her curtains, the sight of her once again pummelling the old Shifty ticker worse than a hundred-yards dash in diver's boots.

What a belter – the image of Bardot in her prime, all tumbling blonde hair and a pair of melons I never stop dreaming about.

Her name's Esme Pickersgill, works on the sweet counter in the local Co-op, a shop I frequent very frequently in the hope that she'll give me a tumble one day, though up to now all I've managed to acquire from her is four hundred packets of Polo mints and a quidsworth of Co-op divi.

Oh, dear, oh dear, there went her nightie.

One thing I adore about Esme is that she's a child of strict routine, does the same thing every single morning – draws back her curtains, has a butcher's up at the sky to see what the weather's doing, takes three steps back, whips her nightie over her head, and embarks on a mind-blowing five minutes of Yoga exercises in the absolute nod.

On second thoughts I'm not at all sure this nature studying of mine is doing me any good at all. It makes me feel like a bloke walking around with a forty-foot flag-pole and nowhere to put it. I shall have to do something very positive about Esme Pickersgill soon or one of these mornings I shall explode all over the room with frustration.

Just look at her go . . . one leg round the back of her neck

7

and the other in the fireplace. Now the deep-breathing bit . . . in . . . out . . . in . . . out . . . her incredible balloons rising and falling like buoys in a heavy swell. Esme, love, stop it before I blow me gasket . . .

BANG! went the door again.

'I've finished, Albert!'

'Ta, mate!'

With one last tremulous eyeful of the heavenly Esme, I stowed away the glasses, slipped on my dressing gown, collected my shaving gear and ventured out onto the landing, doing my best to hide a rampant hard-on with my towel.

Norman, attired in his usual working garb of unwashed khaki shirt and a pair of crumpled blue-jeans which closely resemble the hide of an ageing elephant, was standing in his doorway, attempting to force a comb through the jungle of carrot-coloured hair surmounting his pimply, vacuous features like the fronds of a pineapple.

'Hurry up, Albert, I'm hungry,' he grumbled, wincing as the comb wrenched out a tuft of undergrowth.

'Patience, dear boy, I will not be rushed first thing. It disturbs my metabolical equilibrium.'

He frowned. 'Your wha'?'

'It gets on me tits.'

'Oh.'

'You go ahead if you want to, I'll be down in ten minutes.'

'Nah, I'll wait for you. I don't like having breakfast by meself.'

I smirked knowingly. 'You're scared of Dillys Kranki, that's your trouble.'

I knew he was scared of our landlady's big, butch, black-haired daughter because *every* bloke in the house, including me, was scared of her. She was a nutter – a seventeen-year-old sex-maniac who, while her mother still drew living breath, had as much chance of realising her carnal desires as climbing Everest with her hands tied behind her back.

Oh, I fancied her, all right, big as she was. I mean, there were times up there in my mousehole-in-the-sky, what with Esme Pickersgill tying herself in naked knots and all, that I desired *acutely* the opportunity to die in agony, crushed to death between Dilly's mighty thighs, but the thought of being

8

discovered in the act by her mother was sufficient to quell my most pressing need.

Not for nothing was it rumoured that Frau Kranki had served for five years with the Serbo-Croat cavalry without anyone ever detecting she was not a fella!

Strong? I've seen her clean-and-jerk their solid-oak dining table without so much as taking a preparatory breath *and* hold it aloft while Dillys vacuumed the carpet underneath.

Now, nudging six feet and tipping the scales at thirteen stone myself, I do not regard Albert Shifty as entirely puny, but I tried that dining-table trick after they'd gone and I couldn't even get it off the ground! So, there you have it. Frau Kranki is not, repeat not, a woman to be crossed, and the discovered seduction of Dolly Dillys would most certainly have that disastrous effect.

The trouble is, Dillys's sexual frustration increases hand-in-hand with her mother's diligence, and there are times when Dillys cannot help but come on strong with the men in the house – especially with me – which is why we're all scared of her. For innocent of seduction though we may be, should Momma catch us in a compromising situation with Dillys, I do not doubt we would quickly resemble a pile of bone-splinters you could stuff in a match-box.

Norman's fear, therefore, was most understandable.

'All right, son,' I grinned. 'I won't be two ticks.'

I turned and bounded down the threadbare stairs to the floor below, squeezing into the bathroom just ahead of old man Philby, a retired lay-about who prided himself in never having done an honest day's work in thirty years.

'You're late!' he accused, spearing me with a finger. 'You are encroaching on my bathroom time, Shifty!'

'Oh – you in a tearing hurry to collect your dole, Philby?'

'None of your business, Shifty!'

'Like hell it isn't. It's workers like me who keep you in the idle manner to which you are accustomed, Philby.'

'Shifty by name and shifty by nature – that's you, you . . .'

I closed the door on his tirade and began my ablutions.

Morning, Shifty, I bade the face in the mirror, covering it with shaving soap. Not a bad fizzog, really . . . good crop of dark, curly hair, inherited from my father, and a pair of green

9

Irish eyes, compliments of my mother.

And who might Albert Shifty be, you may be wondering.

Well, he might be the only son of a wealthy stockbroker, heir to a Woking fortune, who, at twenty-two, tired of an over-protected, over-indulged youth of public school, golf, boating, and Mummy's coffee mornings, has fled the fold to experience life in the raw in Frau Kranki's Fulham boarding house.

He might be. But unfortunately he isn't.

Albert Shifty is an only son, all right, but of a devilishly handsome Italian lion-tamer who, twenty-three years ago, while playing to capacity houses on Hampstead Heath, took a raging fancy to a pretty Irish barmaid pulling pints in a local hostelry – and I was the result of his farewell performance.

I was brought up by her parents who live in respectable squalor in Canning Town. I went to school, did all right, left school, got a job with a local builder, learned to do this, that, and quite a bit of the other, realised the builder was making all the money and decided I'd be better off working for myself.

So, here I am.

'Shifty, I protest!' bellowed Philby, thumping the door. 'You are stealing my bathroom time!'

'And you're stealing my hard-earned taxes, Philby! Now, kindly desist the racket or I shall be obliged to nip out and cut your throat!'

The Kranki household was full of nutters like Philby.

On the second floor we've got a mad artist named Fred Van Gogh who paints pictures with egg beaters and knuckle-dusters and things. They're terrible. His name really isn't Van Gogh but he feels it'll give him an edge when he finally gets someone to look at them – which I reckon will be never.

Also on the second floor lives Ernst Von Brik, a German bloke who says he's an inventor, though all I've known him invent is ways of avoiding doing any work. Personally, I think he's an S.S. camp commandant on the run. Frau Kranki thinks the world of him, which seems to support my theory.

On the third floor we've got Harriet Bloom, a highly-inflated, gone-to-seed waitress I reckon used to be on the game before she went to fat. She's got 'that look' in her eye and calls everybody 'dearie'.

Also on the third is Bennie Kenton, a big, randy West Indian bus-driver who's always chuckling with laughter. Norman tells me he caught sight of Bennie naked in the bathroom one morning and swears Bennie's got a dong a foot long – flaccid! Maybe that's what he's always chuckling about.

On the fourth floor there's Harry and Peter Elbert, a couple of outrageous tooty-fruits who claim they're cousins. They have separate rooms but Peter's has hardly been slept in since they moved in six months ago, so Dillys Kranki tells me. She does the cleaning in the house, so she ought to know.

Harry and Peter are students, though what they're studying and where they do it nobody knows. Maybe it's each other.

You might be wondering why I live in such a sleazy dump as this. Well, there are two reasons. The first is that it's dead cheap, and until the Shifty finances improve it's all I can afford. And the second reason is that Frau Kranki is willing, for a modest fee, to let me use her phone number in my business ads and also to take messages for me.

I advertise in the local Putney/Fulham paper once a week and pick up quite a bit of business from it.

The ad. reads:

'Let Albert Do It. Painting. Decorating. All Odd-jobs around the home. No job too small. Sink blocked? Fence falling down? Attic need clearing? Let Albert Do It! Reasonable rates. Satisfaction Guaranteed.'

It's not much of a business but it's all mine and I like it. I've got a clapped-out Ford van that's holding together by the skin of its rivets, a few tools, and Gormless Norman to help me. Who could wish for anything more?

I bloody could, but I'm not likely to get it, so there's no point in wishing.

'Meester Sheefty!'

An imperative Teutonic thump on the bathroom door made me jump so hard I almost had my nose off with the razor. Blimey, it was Frau Kranki. Philby must have shopped me.

'Aha! Good morning, Mrs. Kranki,' I called over-jovially, wondering how it was she always made me feel as though *she* was paying *me* rent. 'Sorry about the delay but . . .'

'Zer iss a telephone call for you!' she barked. 'Kom qvickly!'

'Ohh, lovely – be right there!'

I swilled off the soap, packed up my gear and opened the door. Philby was storming up and down the hall, his complexion matching his puce dressing gown.

'I'll not stand for this, Shifty! I shall protest most strongly to Mrs. Kranki!'

'And I shall tell her I caught you peeping through the key-hole, Philby. They'll take you away and stick electrodes in your brain – if they can find it.'

He made a noise like he'd hit his thumb with a hammer and crashed into the bathroom.

I nipped down one flight of stairs and came face-to-face with the lovely Peter Elbert, sneaking out of Harry's room. Peter's a tall, skinny, blond kid whose big baby-blue eyes give him the appearance of a startled doe.

He looked quite stunning this morning in a dressing gown of powder-blue quilted satin and matching slippers. All that was missing was the throat-scarf and long ivory cigarette-holder and he'd have been dead right for the lead in *Lilac Time*.

'Whoops!' he whooped, blushing to the roots of his tint. 'Sorry, Albert, didn't see you. I w . . . was just going to call Harry.'

'What were you going to call him?' I enquired seriously, pulling his leg.

'Hm? Oh, you . . .' he laughed.

'*Love* the dressing gown, Peter.'

'Do you?' he asked excitedly, firming it about his emaciated torso. 'Yes, I thought it was rather fetching. Harry got one in apple green. So pleased you like it.'

'*Super*. Got to fly – there's a call for me.'

'Oh, good – hope it means lots of money for you.'

I shot down the next flight of stairs, finding Bennie Kenton, our randy bus-driver just ahead of me.

'Morning, Bennie.'

He turned and grinned a snow-blast of teeth. He's a hell of a good-looking fella.

'Hi, man – how's tricks?'

'Thinking up new ones all the time, son. Got to stay ahead of the game, haven't you?'

'Sure, sure, baby.'

'How about you – getting much?'

He chuckled his deep, negro laugh which was answer enough.

I followed him down to the lower hall where he turned left into the gloomy dining room while I continued on to the wall telephone and picked up the dangling receiver.

'Hello . . . ?' I panted.

I heard the crackle of a newspaper and the tinkle of a cup in a saucer, then a female voice asked, 'Is that Albert?'

'Yes, madam – at your service. What can I do for you?'

'I was just reading the local paper and spotted your ad. I was wondering if you installed those loft-ladder things. I've got a big attic and want to use it for storing stuff, but I want a permanent, fold-up ladder . . . you know the kind of thing?'

'Perfectly, madam. I shall be delighted to come round and give you a quote. Where do you live?'

'426 Belview Estate . . . off the Richmond Road, do you know it?'

'Don't worry, I'll find it. What time would be suitable?'

'Could you come this morning – about ten o'clock?'

'Certainly. We'll be there on the dot. Could I have your name, please?'

'It's Pinkerton.'

'Pinkerton . . .' I repeated, jotting it down. 'Would that be "Miss" or "Mrs."?'

She gave a throaty chuckle. 'I thought that was privileged information these days – Women's Lib and all that.'

'Touché,' I concurred. ' "Miz" Pinkerton, then.'

'Ugh, I hate it. It's "Mrs." Pinkerton.'

I was sorry to hear it. She sounded real friendly.

'Right, thank you very much, Mrs. Pinkerton . . . see you at ten.'

As I replaced the receiver I felt a presence behind me but turned too late. Arms like steel hawsers snapped around my chest and crushed the air from my lungs. It was either Dillys Kranki or Guy the Gorilla, and as far as I knew he didn't wear California Poppy perfume at eight thirty in the morning.

'Gotcha!' she hoarsed in my ear.

All I could manage was a throttled gasp.

'You shouldn't come down in your dressing gown!' she whispered voraciously. 'It gets me all horny!'

'Dillys . . . leggo!' I gasped. 'Your mother . . .'

'Screw her!'

Her hand shot inside the gown and found my naked chest. 'Ooh, *lovely* . . .'

'Dillys, get . . . off!'

'Come and see me tonight!'

'Are you mad!'

'Why not?'

'Your mother would beat me to a pulp!'

'She won't know! Creep down after she's gone to bed. She sleeps like a log!'

'No!'

She released me. I turned to her, rubbing my bruised ribs, and found her pouting. She was wearing shrink-wrapped jeans and a white cotton blouse, every seam and button strained to bursting point. With her dark hair captured in two untidy bunches she looked like an Amazon weight-lifter who'd just finished the milking.

'You don't like me,' she sulked, twiddling her fingers.

'Of course I like you, but . . .'

'No you don't – otherwise you'd come and see me.'

'Dillys, your mother would murder me!'

She shook her head. 'No, you don't fancy me.'

'I do, I do! But a fella can't be nipping into his landlady's daughter's room at three in the morning . . . it's just not done!'

She brightened alarmingly. 'I could nip up to yours! Then you couldn't be blamed if . . .'

'No!' I gasped. 'Don't you dare!'

At that moment my right ankle was grabbed in another tug-hawser grip and I looked down to find Fritz, the Kranki dachshund, fucking my leg. He is the randiest little swine on God's earth. For his size it is ludicrous the things he'll have a go at – like six-foot blokes for a start, and he's not averse to raping the sofa when there's nowt else doing.

I've heard that donkeys, proportionate to their size, have the biggest dongs in the animal kingdom, but I reckon Fritz has got them beaten all ends up. He's got a chopper like a frank-furter sausage, huge enough to make a Great Dane shudder. No wonder he's out of his mind with frustration. Any bitch big enough to take him he wouldn't be able to reach!

'Gerroff, you sex maniac!' I hissed, lifting him off the

14

ground with a kick. But even in mid-air he still clung fast, humping away like a clockwork toy.

Dillys was in pleats, her hand over her mouth, stifling laughter. I reckon the sight of Fritz's erection turned her on.

'Dillys, *do* something!'

'He's only doing what comes naturally,' she giggled.

'*That* . . . is not natural! Fritz – gerroff!'

'A few more males around here ought to follow his example,' she grinned, her eyes probing my naked chest. 'Instead of behaving like cold fish.'

'Which is precisely what we'd be if your mother caught us . . . Fritz – *enough*!'

I gave him a shove which sent him skidding backwards across the lino, his little legs scuttling to get purchase on the slippery surface. He didn't make it. Next thing, he slammed into the dinner gong and brought the whole lot down with a terrific crash.

In the same breath, Frau Kranki, all six feet two and fifteen stone of her, peroxide blonde hair snatched back in a severe Germanic bun and pale-blue Arian eyes agleam, appeared in the doorway of the kitchen.

'Vat is goink on here? Dillys – get in here und help me vid da breakfast! Haf you finished your call, Elbert?'

'Yes, Mrs. Kranki.'

'Zen hurry – I don't keep breakfast vaitink for nobody!'

'No, Mrs. Kranki.'

With a sly grin at Dillys, I bolted up the stairs, noting en passant that Fritz was now raping the umbrella stand.

I arrived on the top floor absolutely knackered.

'Where've you bin?' enquired Norman from his doorway. 'I'm starvin'.'

'Had a ph . . . ph . . . fucking hell, these stairs'll kill me . . . phone call. Got an estimate to do for a loft ladder – ten o'clock.'

'Me, too, Albert?'

'Sure.' I entered my room and threw on a clean shirt and a pair of jeans. 'If we get the job she might want us to start right away. Loft ladders are tricky things, I'll need you.'

'Much money in it?'

I grinned evilly. 'A bob or two, mate. I'll convince her to

15

put a bit of flooring in the attic while we're at it, pad the bill a bit.'

'Lovely.'

'Come on, let's get downstairs – the Beast of Belsen's on the warpath. "Hurry up, Elbert, I don't keep breakfast vaitink for nobody!" And watch out for Fritz, he's bang-happy this morning. If you're not careful your right leg'll be giving birth to pups.'

We tumbled down the stairs and into the dining room, decorated Early Mortician. No matter what meal was being served, it always smelled of pickled onions with an undertone of old socks.

They were all there – Fred Van Gogh in his paint-spattered smock and French beret; Ernst Von Brik in his turn-of-the-century grey suit – which was when it had last seen the inside of a dry-cleaners; roly-poly Harriet Bloom in an off-the-shoulder blouse that shouldn't have been; Bennie Kenton, resplendent in his bus-driver's uniform; pale and fragile Harry Elbert in a blue velvet shirt; seated, as always, at his side and practically on his knee – his blond, pale and fragile 'cousin' Peter; and bringing up the rear, his layabout nose buried in the Times, Daniel Philby.

As we arrived, Bennie Kenton looked up from his pre-stressed porridge and opened the bidding with, 'Ah, the workers are with us.'

'Makes a change,' I quipped, for Philby's benefit, and got an affronted sniff in reply.

I sat down in my customary place – next to Bennie, with Norman on my right and Philby next to him. On the opposite side of the long table sat Van Gogh, Von Brik, Harry and Peter. Harriet Bloom occupied the right end position, the left end being reserved for serving.

Frau Kranki was, as usual, in the kitchen and could be seen through the open hatch – which meant she could also see us, which was how she liked things. And Dolly Dillys was to-ing and fro-ing doing the serving.

'Porridge?' she enquired as we sat down.

'Yes, please,' said Norman, who has the constitution of a car-crusher.

I winced, making her laugh. 'A sliver or two of smoked salmon for me, Dillys.'

'Sorry, the smoked salmon's orf.'

'O.K. – quail in aspic.'

I got stale cornflakes, the invariable alternative to porridge.

With the amount of cornflakes consumed in 'Buchenwald' – our nickname for Chez Kranki – it puzzled us why they were always stale. The conclusion we'd reached was that either Frau K. had tapped a continuous source of cut-price stale cornflakes, or had, years before, purchased four hundred tons of them. The other alternative was that she opened all the packets a week in advance and staled them up out of sheer malice.

Dillys hove-to and leaned in with my bowl of flakes, deliberately ramming her left Bristol in my right ear. 'Sugar?' she enquired, reaching into the centre of the table and ramming it in even harder.

'Thank you, Dillys,' I muttered, my nose in the flakes.

'Milk?' she grinned, repeating the process.

It was akin to being deafened by a medicine ball.

'You're too kind.'

'We aim to please. What would you like for afters?'

You, love, I thought, determined to do something about Dillys one of these nights. I mean, how much provocation can a fella stand?

'Eggs and bacon,' I said, and Norman ordered the same.

Away she went, allowing me to sit upright.

'How's the painting coming, Fred?' I asked Van Gogh, who was reading the comic strip in the Daily Mirror.

'Hm?' He looked up, wondering who had addressed him.

'What's the latest project?'

'Ah . . .' he said, setting down his paper, warming to the subject, in fact flattered to hell that somebody had noticed he was in the room. 'Experimentation is everything, Albert – we must drive forward . . . forward all the time, break new territory, not be afraid to cross unfamiliar boundaries. Who said painting must be executed by brush and pallet-knife alone?'

'Who indeed?' I acknowledged, receiving a conspiratorial kick on the foot from Bennie who enjoyed these breakfast-time debates more than he enjoyed accelerating away from a gasping passenger who'd just chased his bus for three blocks. 'So –

17

what is it this time – bicycle chains and false teeth?'

The table laughed.

Van Gogh shook his head. 'No – but you might have some-thing there, I must try those. No, I am currently experimenting with Frau Kranki's carrot-grater.'

'Ja – und I vant it back in time for dinner!' she called through the hatch.

'Madam. I shall be finished by tea-time,' he assured her. 'Once I start I work like a demon.'

'Did you ever do any painting, Harriet?' I asked old Roly Poly.

'Only me toe-nails, dearie – though I did once pose for a mad Italian bloke.'

Bennie gasped in mock-affront. 'Not in the *nude*, I trust.'

She cackled a laugh. 'How else would you pose for an Italian, dear? Randy little cocker-spaniel, he was. Took him three weeks to finish the painting. Then one day I sneaked a look at it and found he'd only bin playing noughts and crosses with himself, dirty devil. He was no more a painter than our cat, it was his way of seducing women.'

'Disgusting,' opinioned Bennie, nudging my knee and whis-pering, 'Hey, man, what a great idea! I'm going to buy me some paints.'

'And paint Harriet?'

He gritted his teeth. 'Are you tryin' to spoil my breakfast?'

'Is it possible?'

He nodded emphatically. 'Yeh! You just did it!'

Up rolled Dillys with our eggs and bacon. 'Two heart-burns, coming up.'

'Dillys,' I tutted, 'that is no way to talk about your mother's cooking.'

'Yes, it is.' She laid my plate before me.

I winced. Frau Kranki is the only woman I know who can make one fried egg and one strip of bacon resemble regurgi-tated Irish stew.

'You still want to argue?' Dillys challenged.

I nudged Norman's arm. 'Please pass the H.P. sauce, the Lea and Perrins, and the mustard.'

Dillys shook her head. 'You'll never make it. I've even tried garlic salt and ground chilli peppers, but that unmistakable flavour still comes through. Why d'you think I eat out?'

'And how's the invention business these days, Herr Von Brik?' I enquired solicitously, rescuing my bacon from drowning in three feet of fat.

'My verk iss top secret, young man,' rapped Von Brik, dunking a hunk of black bread in his own plate of fat and sucking it off with a noise like water rushing down a plug hole. 'Top secret!'

'Excuse me, I didn't mean to pry. It's just that we're all terribly excited by the possibility of your success, aren't we Bennie?'

'Terribly,' nodded Bennie, preoccupied with a close study of what, I'm sure, he hoped was a sausage, hiding beneath his floundering bacon. 'Hey, man . . . you got one of these?'

I high-dived into my gravy and had a feel around. 'No, I . . . ah! There's something here, skulking under the egg. Yes, Benjamin, I do believe it's my lucky day. Love the shirt, Harry.'

Harry smiled bashfully and batted his eyelashes hard enough to cool his coffee. 'Thank you, Albert. We've discovered the dinkiest new boutique in Fulham High Street.'

'Gaywear,' added Peter joyously. 'All super new Italian gear in quite *deva*stating shades.'

Lovely lads.

Don't care what people say, if the world was populated by Harrys and Peters it'd be a lot nicer place. Unusual, granted, but a lot nicer.

At that moment, Norman shattered his burnt toast in a thousand fragments, most of them settling on Philby's porridge like a coating of soot.

'Oh, for Godsake . . . !' snarled Philby.

'Sorry . . .' muttered Norman helplessly. 'It . . . just broke.'

'Perhaps if you buttered it on your plate instead of four feet in the air . . . !' rapped Philby, still smarting from our bathroom encounter.

'Ah, now there's something for you to invent, Herr Von Brik,' I suggested. 'Shatter-proof toast.'

Von Brik scowled darkly and sucked up another mouthful of dripping. 'I sink zer iss too much talk at breakfast time. I sink ve should just eat and shaddup!'

'That's your fault, Norman,' I said. 'The noise of your shattering toast disturbs Herr Von Brik's thought processes. Why don't you dunk your bread like he does, it'd make for much quieter living all round.'

Sluuuurrrrpppp! went Von Brik for a third time.

'See what I mean?' I said, and Bennie choked on his coffee.

'How's the bus-driving business, Bennie?' I asked him.

'Great, mate. Collected two cripples on a pedestrian crossing and a seeing-eye dog having a pee at a bus-stop this week. Splat! Lovely.'

'How many points was that?'

'Fifty.'

'You'll have to watch it, they'll be making you an inspector.'

'What – and get me out of the cab? Never. I'd run over meself first.'

Philby shook out his paper angrily. 'I think your conversation is obscene, Mister Kenton – not at all funny.'

'Oh, go on with you,' chided Harriet Bloom. 'Where's your sense of humour, Mister Philby?'

'He saves it for the dole queue,' offered Bennie. 'He must laugh himself sick every time he draws our hard-earned money.'

Philby slammed down his paper, thrust back his chair, and stormed from the room.

'Oops, now you've done it,' sniggered Peter. 'You two are awful.'

'I entirely agree vid Herr Philby,' announced Von Brik, also jumping to his feet. 'Ze conversation at zis table iss purile, imbecilic und repulsive. I bid you goot mornink, madam.'

He bowed stiffly to Harriet and slammed his heels together, forgetting he was wearing carpet-slippers. He winced with pain as his ankles collided, then stalked off with a barely-contained goose-step.

'You ought to behave better at the breakfast table,' I told Bennie. 'You're frightening all the guests away.'

'So why haven't you left, man?'

I shrugged. 'Because I'm purile, imbecilic and repulsive.'

'More coffee anyone?' invited Dillys, bringing the percolator over.

Bennie feigned surprise. 'You mean that bean isn't finished yet, Dillys?'

'It's in its death-throws, but I can squeeze a drop more. Any takers?'

There were none.

'Chickens,' she sneered.

'Well . . .' I sighed, patting my stomach, 'another sumptuous repast to your mother's credit. I just don't know how she maintains the standard morning after morning. I can hardly bear to tear myself away from the table. Tomorrow, though, I think I'll try a *boiled* egg.'

'I wouldn't,' muttered Van Gogh. 'I had one last week and couldn't lift an arm for three days. That must have been one constipated chicken.'

'Oh. Er . . . scrambled, then?'

Harriet Bloom gasped. 'What are you – a masochist?'

I shrugged. 'Omelette?'

Everybody fell about laughing.

'For pity's sake . . .' I cried dramatically, '. . . *what*, then?'

'Do what I do,' suggested Dillys. 'Eat out.'

'Come on, Norman,' I said, 'we have work to do.'

'Aw, just one more piece of toast, Albert.'

'No, you've shattered three, that's your quota. Happy painting, Fred. You ought to try committing a Frau Kranki breakfast to canvas . . . call it Nagasaki, Mon Amour or Reflections From The Somme, you'd make a million. Happy driving, Bennie – listen, you ought to switch to the Wimbledon Park route, there's an old people's home along there, worth two hundred points a week at least.'

'Sick, that,' said Bennie, hiding his bacon under his egg and covering the lot with his paper napkin.

'Happy studying, Harry and Peter,' I said, getting up.

'Toodle-oo, Albert,' smiled Harry.

'Ciao, Albert,' said Peter, wiggling the fingers of his free hand, his other lost under the table, presumably holding Harry's. 'Good luck with the job.'

'Bye bye, dearie,' I winked at Harriet. 'Happy waitressing.'

'That'll be the day,' she sneered.

Frau Kranki popped her head through the hatch, resembling for a moment a wall-mounted water-buffalo. 'Don't be late for dinner, Elbert – seven sharp!'

'What are we having, Mrs. Kranki?'

'Stuffed sheep's heart and sauerkraut.'

My stomach churned.

'Oh! I've just remembered – I've got an appointment to-night. Regrettably I shall have to forego dinner, what a shame, still you can't win 'em all.' I turned to Norman. 'Come on, son.'

Dillys had positioned herself in the doorway for our exit, forcing me to squeeze past her.

'See you tonight, then,' she whispered, her hand trickling across my thigh as I ran the gauntlet.

'No!'

'I'll be up at three.'

'No!'

She shrugged. 'Okay – two. I know the waiting will be hell for you . . .' she winked sexily, '. . . but *so* worthwhile.'

I squeezed past into the hall and was immediately set-upon by Fritz who had been waiting to rape my left leg. Clunk! I stopped him dead in his tracks with a toe in the throat and sent him yipping into the kitchen.

'What's up wiv him?' asked Norman.

'He's got lover's nuts,' I told him. 'Come on, we're going to be late.'

CHAPTER TWO

The bloke who named it Belview Estate either had a wicked sense of humour or he was kinky about gasworks, because that was the only view immediately apparent as we drove into the estate.

'Where the 'ell's number 426 in this lot, d'you suppose?' asked Norman.

'Roughly somewhere between 425 and 427,' I ventured, scanning the houses.

They went on for miles, row after row of identical grey-rendered boxes, each with its garage and neat little front lawn. These estates always make me think that the builder produced the houses out of a machine and that he'd gone on his hols and forgotten to switch it off. Plop . . . plop . . . plop . . . six hundred too many by the time he'd got back.

On we drove, along Rosethorn Road, into Acacia Avenue, turning right into Daisychain Drive . . .

'Nice little houses,' remarked Norman.

'Nice,' I acknowledged.

'Nice little gardens.'

'Little,' I agreed.

Everybody and her sister were out in the sunshine, weeding the garden, washing the car, pegging out clothes and almost every bird we spotted paused in her labour to give us a glance, the presence of a strange van conceivably constituting the highlight of her day.

'What a life,' I muttered. 'They're all in prison and they don't know it.'

'Hm?' grunted Norman. 'Whatcha mean, Albert?'

'Suburban solitary confinement, son – they're all doing porridge as sure as though they were in Holloway. They're chained to the walls by kids, debts and absentee husbands, poor cows. Ask any one of them and she'll tell you she's going out of her mind with boredom.'

'Hm?' he frowned. 'They look happy enough to me.'

'That's because the sun's shining. But drive round here on

23

the seventy-second consecutive rainy day and ask them. You'd find half of them in bed with the vapours.'

'Nah,' he grinned.

'All right, we'll ask Mrs. Pinkerton.'

'Who's she?'

'The bird we're going to see! Hey up, there's number 398, we're getting warm . . .'

We found number 426 just where I said it'd be. Leaving Norman to guard the van, I hopped out, went up the concrete driveway and rang the bell. Chimes donged in the hall. I had a look around./ Neat little garden, but no plastic gnomes in sight, thank God. I wiggled my fingers at Norman and he wiggled his back.

I heard the door behind me open. I turned . . .

By gum, she was a little cracker, blonde, nice face, dreamy eyes – and stacked. My eyes automatically dropped down her façade. Blimey, she was wearing shorts, *very* shorts, and sticking out of the bottoms were two of the shapeliest legs I'd drooled over in a long time. She was lovely.

Age? Oh . . . early twenties going on fifty-four sexually. She had a very naughty smile.

'Hi,' she beamed, working me over with the eyes which did a lightning fast trip up and down *my* façade before finally coming to rest in my eyes.

'Albert, I presume.'

I gave a little bow, knowing I was in friendly territory. 'Albert Shifty – at your undivided service. Mrs. Pinkerton, I presume?'

'Who else?'

She stood back to allow me through. As I passed close to her a drift of perfume slid up my nose and blew the transistors in my brain, leaving me a mangled mess. Being a fatalistic sort of chap I gave myself up to the situation and decided to enjoy it, job or no job. Come to think of it, who gave a stuff about an old loft ladder!

'Beautiful day,' I ventured as she closed the door.

'Fantastic. I was sunbathing in the garden when you rang. It's not often we get the chance, is it?' She gave me a wonderfully friendly smile. 'Well, I suppose you'd like to see it?'

Christ! would I?

She led off along the little hallway, stopping my breath with an eyeful of gorgeous bottom packaged in those short, short shorts, then completely destroyed my equilibrium by mounting the stairs.

I gave her a three-tread lead then followed, my eyes losing focus at the panorama of her twitching buttocks, nakedly visible up the legs of the shorts.

'I have so much stuff to store,' she said conversationally, 'I just don't know where to put it.'

I do, love.

'So, I thought about the attic. Trouble is it's such a drag bringing the ladder in from the garden every time you want to go up there for a suitcase of something . . .'

'Quite agree,' I agreed, not knowing what the hell I was saying. Where was the lucky Mister Pinkerton, I wondered. Perhaps he'd died from exhaustion. I imagined a frail, white-haired twenty-six-year-old physical wreck lying in hospital with a drip-feed up his nose, begging them to keep her away from him. 'No more . . . no more! She's insatiable!'

'Well, here we are . . .' she sighed, reaching the landing and turning abruptly, so that, three treads below, my face was level with her Y-front. She looked up and pointed, her yellow floral blouse riding high and exposing a stretch of coffee-tanned belly.

'Oh, yes . . .' I said, as though I'd never seen a loft hatch before. 'Very nice.'

'Would you like to inspect it? I've got some small steps in the cupboard here.'

'Yes . . . yes, I think I'd better.'

She went to the cupboard and I was close behind her, light-headed in the wake of her perfume. 'Here, let me . . .'

I got the steps out, set them up under the loft hatch and climbed up. She, I noticed, came round to the front as though to hold the ladder, taking up a position of extreme intimacy, her chin almost on my knee.

I pushed up the hatch and stuck my head through the hole, noting the position of the rafters. 'Yes . . . everything looks fine. I see no difficulties.'

'What's up there? You know, we've been in this house for three years and I've never seen the attic.'

Aha! *'We've'* been in this house, she'd said. So there *was* a Mister Pinkerton around somewhere.

'You *haven't?'* I frowned down at her. 'Oh, you've missed a treat. Come up and take a look.'

I shot down the steps.

'Well, I . . .' she hesitated, though her heart wasn't in it. 'I hate ladders.'

'No need to worry, I'll hold it for you.'

Any time.

'Come on . . . up you go.'

Cautiously she mounted the steps, suddenly running out of ladder to hold on to.

'Here . . .' I said, offering my hand.

She took it, the touch of hers sending shock-waves of delight through me.

'Go on – reach up for the hole,' I urged her.

Wobblingly, she stood upright and made a grab for the lip of the hatch, caught it, then climbed another step, releasing my hand.

'Oooh, it's awfully dark up here . . .'

'Let your eyes adjust to the light, it takes a few seconds.'

I was wishing it'd take a couple of hours, because from where I was standing I could see right up the legs of her shorts and the sight of her yellow bikini knicks and the bulge of her pubic mound was doing wonders for the metabolism. Knocking hell out of the heart, maybe, but just great for the arteries.

'There's lots of useful space up here, Albert.'

Extremely useful, angel, and I know just how to fill it.

'Indeed there is. I think you're right to make use of it.'

'I'm coming down now, where's your hand?'

I gave it to her.

'Phew, thank you . . .' she panted, like she'd just made it down the Matterhorn. 'Well, what d'you think? Will it be expensive?'

'Well, the loft ladder itself is about forty pounds. I'll have to rebuild the hatch-cover to open downwards, and the installation itself is a bit tricky. It's difficult to say how long it would take, but I couldn't finish it in one day. Let's say . . . ten hours' labour – including the collection of the ladder – at five pounds an hour, that's fifty pounds, making a total of ninety.'

'Hm . . . well, that sounds reasonable. When could you start?'

I gave a shrug. 'Right this minute if you like.'

She thought about it, then gave an emphatic nod. 'Right – you've got yourself a deal.'

'Thanks very much,' I grinned. 'We'll do a good job for you.'

She gave me the eyes again. 'Yes, I'm sure you will.'

I turned to go, but hesitated and swung back to her. 'I . . . I wonder if you'd like to consider putting in a bit of flooring while we're doing the job. It'd make things much easier for you to walk around up there. If you accidentally trod between the rafters you'd come right through the ceiling, you know.'

'Oh, dear . . . well, how much would it cost?'

'I could put down a few sheets of chipboard. They come eight feet by four at five pounds each. How about six of those, that'd be plenty.'

'Thirty pounds . . .' she mused, then nodded. 'All right, if you recommend it.'

'I do.'

'Fine – carry on.'

I preceded her down the stairs to the front door.

'Thank you very much, Mrs. Pinkerton . . . you may now return to your sunbathing and leave everything in our hands. We shall be back within the hour with the stuff.'

'Right,' she laughed. 'Got to stock up on the tan, I'm off to Majorca next week. Don't want to arrive lily-white.'

'You – lily-white? You've got a fabulous tan already.'

So help me, she lifted the hem of her blouse and inspected her belly. 'Well . . . not bad, but I want more than this.'

'Right – back to the spit. When we return I'll come round the back so's not to disturb you.'

'How very thoughtful,' she smiled, reaching for the door-knob.

Not at all, love – I want an eyeful of you in your bikini!

*   *   *

I got it, too.

We were back within the hour, complete with loft-ladder and the sheets of chipboard which I'd sawn down the middle in order to get them through the loft-hole.

27

Leaving Norman in the van, I went up the side of the house towards the rear lawn, tingling with anticipation at seeing Pinkerton again and wondering if I'd have the good fortune to catch her flaked out in her bikini.

As I reached the end of the house, I slowed and softened my footfall, then gingerly stuck my head round the corner. Whoops! there went the old ticker again. She was there, all right, sprawled in a sun-chair on a little patio, eyes closed, lapping up the hot sun like a thirsty pussycat, cute as Christmas in a tiny yellow bikini that covered everything and hid nothing.

I have never ceased to wonder about this bikini business. Here was a bird, lying around in full public gaze, ninety-nine and nine-tenths stark naked, and not giving a stuff. And the same went for millions of other birds on hundreds of beaches every summer. Yet if you happened to inadvertently catch them in their pyjamas, which hid everything, they'd throw a bleeding fit and dash around in demented circles, trying to escape.

Balmy.

Still, ours is not to reason why, ours is to thank God they haven't tumbled to it yet.

Oh, what a sight she was, all tanned satin skin and tumbling blonde hair, all graceful curves and delicious bumps. She looked so damn good I felt a terrific urge to rush over and throw meself on top of her, grab a great mouthful of those delectable lips and to hell with the consequences.

What, I wondered, would the consequences be? Would she scream blue murder and fight like a lynx? Or grab me by the hair and murmur huskily, 'What the hell took you so long?'

There are times when I wish I was not so disturbed by women. I reckon if I spent only half the time that I devote to thoughts of their seduction to business I'd be a multi-millionaire by now. Still, you can't deny your nature can you? If you love 'em, you love 'em, and that's all there is to it.

Well, I was getting sore eyes and a few other things standing there ogling this beauty, so I thought I'd better make a bit of noise and wake her up. So, backing up a few steps, I stamped around a bit and whistled a few bars of *I'm In The Mood For*

Love, then came round the corner at a brace of knots, expecting to find her hurriedly slipping on her blouse.

Nothing of the kind.

Apart from raising a languid hand to bid me welcome, she didn't stir a muscle. 'Hi . . . you're back,' she smiled, shielding her eyes with her hand. 'Get everything?'

I approached gingerly, not quite knowing where to put my eyes. By God, she was a cool one. Not the slightest sign of embarrassment. Just lay there calm as you please, showing me all that flesh and those fantastic melons.

'Yes, no problems,' I said, drawing close. 'Sorry if I disturbed you, you look so comfortable there.'

'It's fabulous. I'm a real sun-worshipper.'

'That's obvious,' I grinned. 'You'll have all the other girls in Majorca gnashing their teeth with envy. The fellas, of course, will be gnashing their teeth for quite another reason.'

She laughed, delighted by the compliment. Well, I thought I'd try it, see what reaction I got.

'Have you been to Majorca?' she asked, her mouth still holding the smile.

I shook my head. 'Nah . . . I'd like to, though. Maybe next year.'

'You'd love it. You look the sun-sand-and-sea type.'

'Oh?' I said, the pulse leaping a bit at the personal drift of the chat. 'What type is that?'

She gave a little shrug. 'Oh . . . out-doorsy . . . very fit. Do you swim?'

'Like a shark,' I grinned.

More like a bleeding brick if the truth were known. I can't *stand* water.

'It shows,' she said, giving me a quick all-over flash.

I had to cough to clear the throat. 'Yes, well . . . I'd better get cracking . . .'

She made to get up. 'I'll go through and open the front door for you.'

'Oh, thanks . . .'

I didn't move. I stayed right where I was and let her walk past me, to the rear door, everything exploding as she came up close, every pore and dimple of her oil-slicked body microscopically mine. How I restrained myself from grabbing hold

29

of her I do not know, but I reckoned she knew it was a close thing.

As she reached the door she turned, her eyes hooded, then, with humorous censure, she pointed to the corner of the house, indicating I should be on my way.

'Oh . . . yes,' I grinned, and as I started off, she opened the door and disappeared through it.

Well, I was finished for the day, wasn't I? I mean, what red-blooded lad could concentrate on installing a blinking loft-ladder knowing there was a fantastic-looking, near-naked blonde sun-bathing out back in the garden? *And* not only that, but a blonde who was obviously ripe for a bit of a flirt to help while away a boring old afternoon.

'Everythin' okay?' enquired Norman when I reached the van.

'Better than okay, son – bleeding marvellous. Come on, let's get this gear inside.'

'Whatcha mean "marvellous"?' he frowned.

'Because everything *is* marvellous!' I declared expansively, with a sweep of my arms. 'It's a beautiful day, Norman, a fantastic day . . . and we are working, earning bread . . . the sky is blue, the dear little birds are singing their hearts out . . . and I have just been chatting a fantastic piece of grumble who is patently not averse to chatting me back.'

His eyes popped. 'No kiddin'!'

'I kid you not, it's all systems go. She is lying back there clad only in a couple of hankies and did not flinch so much as a twitch when I hove-to a few minutes ago.'

'Cor . . .' he gasped. 'You mean she just lay there and . . . cor . . .' He licked his lips and swallowed hard. 'Hey, d'you reckon I could get a butcher's, Albert?'

'Despicable youth,' I sneered. 'What a cess-pit for a mind you have. Must I remind you that you are here to work, not fill that foul receptacle of a bird-brain with visions of noddified pulchritude.'

'Ah, Albert . . .' he pouted.

'Well . . . perhaps just one peep,' I relented. 'In lieu of wages.'

'Ah, Albert . . .' he protested.

'Well, we'll see, depends on how hard you work. Come on, Shiftless, get this stuff inside.'

He set about the task with a gusto quite foreign to his nature, and within minutes we were knocking hell out of the loft hatch.

*   *   *

'D'you reckon she's out there now?' whispered Norman. He was down below me, holding the hatch cover, while I, up the step ladder, was driving screws into its new hinges.

'Haven't given it a thought,' I lied. 'I suppose so, yes.'

He gazed furtively around. 'Hey, Albert . . . how about taking a peek from that bedroom window?'

I gasped, appalled, and followed his pointing finger to the open door of a rear bedroom.

'I reckon we'd be looking right down on her from in there,' he hoarsed gleefully, the light of unaccustomed animation brightening his eyes.

'Dirty, that, Norman,' I protested. 'That's voyeurism of the worst kind. Besides which, to enter the private domain of a bedroom unbidden is unprincipled trespass and a flagrant contravention of our business ethics.'

'Sure. Shall I go first or will you?'

I stepped smartly down from the ladder. 'We'll go together.'

Now I sprang to the banisters and hung over them, listening for sounds in the house. Silence.

'Right, mate . . .'

We slipped into the bedroom, a fluttery, feathery, feminine room that held her perfume. It made me go funny in the head.

'Cor, just look at that bed,' gasped Norman, wide-eyed. 'Ee, just imagine her lying sprawled out there . . .'

'Desist, you beast,' I chided, resenting him stealing my very thought.

Cautiously I approached the window and sneaked a look down. By gum, there she was, lying, as Norman had predicted, immediately below us, her head pointing to the house so that we now viewed her upside down, a most provocative angle.

Hot breath disturbed the curtain as Norman came alongside, then even hotter breath gushed out in a rush as he clapped eyes on the miracle below.

'By the . . . cringe!' he exclaimed hoarsely, and fell into a concentrated, gaping study.

It was a full half-minute before he finally managed, in a low, wondering tone, 'Ohh, Albert . . . just look at it . . .'

'What d'you think I'm doing – peeling grapes?'

'I'd love to peel her grapes, Albert – or rather her grape-*fruits*. Oooh, just think of rippin' that bikini off her and . . . gettin' right in there and . . . you know somethin', Albert?'

'What, old comrade?'

'If you nearly close your eyes she looks stark naked.'

'I've got mine nearly closed.'

'Oh. Well, she does, doesn't she?'

'Damn right.'

'D'you really fancy it, Albert?'

'Like a monkey fancies nuts, Norman.'

'Going to do anything about it, then?'

'Like what?'

'Like letting her know, for a start.'

'I reckon she knows already.'

'Well, then . . .'

'Well, then – what?'

'Well, get stuck in, then.'

'Norman, you do not just "get stuck in" to someone else's missus!'

'But you said she gave you the come-on.'

'I did not. I said she was not averse to a bit of chat. There's a chasm of difference between a bored bird desiring a flirty chat and ripping her knickers off.'

'Yeh . . .' he sighed. 'You reckon she's bored, then?'

'Norman, I am not Fantasto, The Mind Reader. How should I know whether she's bored or not? She might be very happily married and simply enjoying the sunshine till her old man gets home.'

'Lucky bugger,' he sighed again. 'Just think of it . . . every night they come up here into this room . . . she whips it all off and climbs between those very sheets . . . he climbs in after her . . . grabs hold of all that lovely hot flesh . . . sinks his mush between those beautiful boobs . . . then she opens up and he sinks his . . .'

'Norman, desist! . . . I beg you,' I added weakly. 'Come on,

32

let's get back to the job, it'll take your mind off it.'

'Some hope.'

'Yeah, I know.'

It was about an hour later. Norman was up in the loft and I was on the ladder, both of us screwing the securing frame of the loft-ladder to the rafters, when I heard the cheerful tinkle of ice in glasses emanating from the hall below.

'Hi, up there!' she called.

I looked down, in time to cop an over-head shot of a bursting bra as she mounted the stairs. She now had her blouse and shorts on again.

'Warm work?' she smiled.

'Like an oven,' I exaggerated, wiping my brow.

'Thought you might like a little refreshment – it's fresh lime and soda.'

As she reached the landing I climbed down from the steps. 'That's very kind of you, Mrs. Pinkerton.'

She looked far too young to be called Mrs. anything.

She looked up and caught sight of Norman's head sticking down through the hole. 'Hello . . .'

'My assistant, Mister Norman,' I said. 'Stay up there, Norman, I'll pass your drink up.'

He scowled but obeyed.

'How's it coming?' she asked.

Any second now, I thought.

'Oh, fine . . . we've re-hung the hatch cover, now we're installing the frame which holds the ladder. When it's finished, all you have to do is pull down the trap door and the ladder slides out with it, then slides back again when you close it.'

'How very clever,' she said, making me feel like Einstein.

'How's the sun-bathing coming along?' I asked. Daft question but I wanted her to stay.

'Great, it's really hot out there. Wish I had a swimming pool.'

'I'll put one in for you – for free,' I grinned. 'Provided I can come and use it.'

'*That* . . . is a deal,' she laughed.

'Yes, well maybe *Mister* Pinkerton might have a word or two to say about that.'

She didn't say anything, just maintained the smile and kept

33

looking up at the hole in the ceiling. 'Well, I'll leave you to it. You'll be stopping work for lunch, I presume?'

'Just a quick sandwich. We'll nip into Putney at one o'clock, be back at two.'

'My, you are conscientious,' she said, heading for the stairs.

'Like my ad. says – I guarantee satisfaction.'

'That's good to know,' she laughed, over her shoulder.

She reached the bottom of the stairs and started across the hall, then, just before she disappeared from my view, she threw a glance upwards, the smile in her eyes belting me under the heart. Then she was gone.

'Woooo . . . ow!' gasped Norman, up aloft. 'Is she something!'

I shrugged. 'Not much.'

'You're kidding!'

With a sigh I turned and mounted the steps. 'Of course I'm kidding, you berk . . .' I snatched up the screw-driver and drove home a number eight with verve. 'Norman, remind me never again to work for a bikini-ed bird on a hot summer day.'

'Oh? Does it disturb your metabolic equilibrium, then, Albert?'

'No,' I said, driving in another screw. 'It escalates my *Fritz* syndrome something 'orrible.'

'Christ,' he sighed, 'another one to learn. Why can't you have things everybody else has?'

*   *   *

We knocked off, reluctantly, at one and headed for the Wimpey in Putney High Street, which was hot, smelly and altogether unbearable, a condition aggravated by a waitress of similar disposition.

'Yers?' she enquired solicitously, flopping a soaking-wet J-Cloth onto the table and giving it a lethargic wipe.

'Hamburger, medium rare, no onions, garnished with lettuce and tomato, the bun toasted to a rich golden brown . . . and may I see the wine list, please,' I cracked.

'Smart arse,' she muttered, flicking somebody's crumbs into my lap.

'Same for me,' said Norman. 'With two coffees, please.'

'Two?' she grimaced.

'One's for him.'

'Ain't he got a tongue?'

'Oh, yes. Albert, show the lady your tongue.'

I did so and got a side-swipe with the J-Cloth. 'Cheeky monkeys, I'll call the manager!'

She trolled off, bad on her feet, poor thing.

'I reckon she fancies you,' observed Norman.

'Too bad. I'm already spoken for by Harriet Bloom.'

'Nah, not *her* . . . I mean Mrs. Pinkerton.'

'Pardon?'

'I reckon she's got the hots for you.'

'Don't be ridiculous.'

'No, I mean it, Albert.'

'And what, O Wise One, leads you to that preposterous conclusion?'

'Well . . . the way she looks at you. Those eyes . . .'

'She looks at everyone that way; it's the way they're shaped.'

'Knackers, she fancies you all right, I can tell.'

'Norman,' I sighed, 'would that you were right. Nothing would give me greater consolation than to leap into Mrs. P and swim upstream for an hour or two, but I fear romantic wish-fulfilment is clouding your tiny mind to the sad facts of reality. She is a married woman and . . .'

'Since when did that stop them having it off with the milk-man?'

'True.'

'And you said yourself they were all climbing the walls with loneliness and boredom on those estates.'

'True again, Norman, but . . .'

He didn't interrupt, which left me floundering a bit.

'Nah . . .' I shook my head. 'It'd be too good to be true.'

'But it does happen, doesn't it?'

'Well . . . yes.'

'Well, I think it's happening to you,' he said emphatically.

His sureness excited me. Could he really be right? Was the delectable Pinkerton within my grasp? The possibility sickened me with jubilation.

'Well . . . let's see what happens this afternoon,' I said. 'I shall play it for all it's worth and see what happens.'

'Don't worry about me, Albert, I'll get the bus home.'

35

I grinned at him, quite touched by his concern. 'You're a good lad, Norman. I must think about paying you some wages . . . sometime.'

'What – and spoil a beautiful relationship?' he smiled. 'Hey up, here comes laughing Lil.'

Down crashed our hamburgers and coffees, more in the saucers than in the cups. 'Anythin' else?'

'Er, yes . . .' I said, 'Crepes suzette et gáteau Feuilleté á la Confiture, miss . . . twice.'

'You cheeky monkey!' she spat, taking another swipe at me before storming off.

'What was that you ordered?' gaped Norman.

I shrugged. 'Buggered if I know, read it in a book once. Nobody ever seems to have it.'

*   *   *

We got back at two. I rang the door bell but got no reply, so I whipped round the back, hoping to find her supine again, but ran into disappointment – in a way. She was standing at the fence talking to a neighbour – but what a neighbour! A tall, slender, dark-haired bird, a bit like Jackie Onassis but not so angular, nor, I suspected, *quite* so rich.

At my arrival, the dark-haired bit told Pinkerton who swung round and gave me the friendly wave that had now become an integral part of our relationship.

'Hi . . .' she called, beaming her friendly smile.

I walked across the lawn, acknowledging the dark piece with a smile and a nod, noting, as I drew close, that she had stupendous grey eyes and a glint in them not unlike Pinkerton's.

'Hello,' she said, arching a cute brow.

'This is Mrs. Lambert,' Pinkerton said. 'I've been telling her all about you . . .'

'Oh?' I grinned. 'And she's still prepared to talk to me?'

They both laughed, their eyes flashing girl-to-girl signals at each other, Mrs. Lambert's saying to Pinkerton's, 'I see what you mean'.

'Mrs. Lambert may be interested in a loft-ladder, too,' explained Pinkerton. 'She'd like to come and see the finished product.'

'Lovely. As I told Mrs. Pinkerton, I guarantee satisfaction.'

Lambert smiled, making dimples. 'So she told me. It's good to know someone does these days.'

I shrugged. 'Well, it's only good business, isn't it? If I do a good job on . . . pardon me, I mean *for* Mrs. Pinkerton, maybe she'll recommend me to others.'

The slip was intentional, and it went home, causing another secretive exchange of glances and a concealed snigger.

A right couple, these two, didn't miss a trick.

'I just *am* recommending you,' insisted Pinkerton. 'What more can a girl do?'

'Thank you,' I said, 'I appreciate it. Now, if you'll let me in, we'll continue the good work. Nice meeting you, Mrs. Lambert.'

'You'll be seeing me again soon.'

Promises, promises.

Pinkerton accompanied me across the lawn to the rear door. 'She's a good friend,' she told me. 'Don't know what I'd do without her. She makes life here bearable.'

'Oh? What's the problem, Mrs. Pinkerton?'

'Same problem as on all the other big estates – galloping boredom.'

Twang.

'Oh, really? Why don't you both go out to work?'

'Our husbands don't approve.'

'Oh.'

We'd reached the door. 'Go round, I'll let you in,' she said.

'Good thing you have her to talk to, then,' I persisted.

She gave a wry smile. 'Without Angela they would have carted me off in a straight-jacket months ago, believe me.'

'Shame. Well, I hope we've brought a bit of interest to your life,' I joked. 'Maybe I'll use that as my slogan in future. "Keep Suburban Blues At Bay – Install A Swinging Loft-Ladder Today!"'

She laughed brightly. 'Hey, that's very good! . . . and nearer the truth than you think. Go on, I'll let you in.'

In the afternoon things got worse – or better, because around three o'clock we discovered Angela Lambert had joined Pinkerton on the patio, doubling our torment.

Deciding to risk another squint from the bedroom window, Norman and I crept in and peered down, suffering mild heart attacks at the sight of not one but *two* bikini-ed lovelies pegged out on their sun-beds, Angela Lambert sporting a navy-blue floral G-string bikini of such miniscule proportions she really needn't have bothered.

'Christ, who's *that*!' gasped Norman.

'Bird next door,' I muttered, deeply preoccupied with visually gobbling Angela Lambert's lovely body. 'By the cringe, Norm, there's more meat down there than in Smithfield Market.'

'Aye – *and* better hung. Ee, I don't half fancy the dark piece, Albert. I'd like to fling meself out of this window and land upside down on her stomach, with my face buried deep in her . . .'

'Norman! Oh, uncouth youth . . .'

'Well, wouldn't you?'

'Not half. Hey up, it's time to baste the roast.'

Angela Lambert had sat up and was reaching for the sun oil. Pouring out a handful, she started on her long, slender legs, did those, then lay down and started on her stomach. Round and round she went, the tips of her fingers sliding into the top of her knicks and at one point giving us a quick flash of dark pubic hair.

'Cor!' gasped Norman. 'Did you see that!'

'No,' I gulped, sweating copiously.

Now she sat up again and began basting her chest, freely plunging her hand into her tiny bra from time to time to ensure total coverage.

'Aw, Albert . . .' groaned Norman.

'Steady, son, steady . . . Norman?'

'Yes, Albert?'

'Remind me never *ever* to travel without my binoculars in future.'

'Yes, Albert.'

'What an opportunity.'

'I could go back and get them!' he suggested eagerly.

I shook my head. 'Time is pressing, we must get on. But tomorrow, by God . . .'

Reluctantly taking our leave, we returned to the attic and continued the slog, the project now of very secondary importance and occupying none of our concentration whatever.

'Ee, Albert,' said Norman, sighing wistfully for the umpteenth time, 'it must be wonderful to have a bird like either of them. How proud you'd feel walking down the street with them, takin' them to the pictures . . .' he gave a dirty chuckle, '. . . to say nothin' of climbing into the sack with 'em. Ee, just imagine them lyin' there in the nod, begging for it . . . all silky flesh and smelling like Harrod's scent counter. Imagine doin' it to Mrs. Pinkerton in the bath . . . or ravishin' the dark one on a sheepskin rug in front of the fire . . .'

'Couple of screws, Norman.'

'You can say that again – a right pair of . . .'

'Norman – please pass me a couple of screws!'

'Oh. Ever had a bird in a bath, Albert?'

'Only my rubber duck, Norman.'

'Garn, bet you have. Bet you've had hundreds of birds in your time. You must've met the odd little raver on this job, haven't you – before I started working for you?'

'Norman, you would not be*lieve* the situations I have encountered,' I lied, pandering to his need for vicarious titillation. 'I recall most vividly the case of the vicar's daughter who fleetingly – and almost disastrously – entered my life a year ago this very month.'

'Go on,' he breathed, wide-eyed. 'What happened?'

'It was a sash-window job – huge old vicarage in Wimbledon, overlooking the common. Beautiful weather, very hot. I was working away in one of the bedrooms, mending the sash-window. The sun was beating into the room, so I took my shirt off to cool down and tan up. Suddenly I heard a sound behind me . . . I turned . . . and discovered a girl standing in the doorway, watching me.'

'Cor . . .' he gasped. 'What was she like?'

'Awful. Real Plain Jane . . . untidy hair, awful frock, but a nice, vicar's daughter type of face, sort of pure, angelic, if you know what I mean.'

'Sure. How old?'

'Oh . . . seventeen . . . eighteen.'

'Body?'

I shook my head. 'Non-existent. At least, none immediately evident beneath that bell-tent of a dress. I think it was her mother's.'

39

'Go on – what happened?'

'Not much – at first. I said hello and she gave me a bashful smile and asked me if I minded her watching me. I said I didn't and she moved closer, then very close. We got talking. Nice kid . . . lovely voice, very softly spoken. We chatted about this and that. She told me she was an only child and got a bit lonely in the big old house, spent a lot of her time reading in her room, which was next to the one I was working in. I asked her what she liked reading and she said Proust, Goldsmith, Dickens . . .'

'Who?'

'Quite. Ho, a real little swinger, I thought. Well, the afternoon wore on, I finished the job, then she asked me if I'd take a look at a cupboard door in her room, said it wouldn't close properly. Of course I said I would and in we went. Well, I went straight to the cupboard door and opened it . . . and got the shock of my life. Inside the cupboard were shelves, and lying on one of the shelves, open at the centre-fold was a copy of . . .'

'Yes, what?' he breathed.

'*Playgirl.*'

His eyes popped. 'No!'

'Damn right. And the centre-fold picture was of a huge negro with a dangle four times longer and eight times thicker than Bennie's!'

'Jezuswept . . .'

'Straight up.'

'What happened then?'

'I heard the door being locked. I shot round, found her leaning against the door, smiling a smile that really blew my fuse. She'd undergone a complete transformation, Norman . . . Gone was the sweet, naive vicar's daughter and in her place stood a she-cat, a temptress, a sexual Amazon radiating unimaginable promiscuous promise.'

'Aw, Albert . . .' he croaked, sweating freely. 'It's a dream come true.'

I shook my head. 'More like a nightmare, old son. Little did I realise in those first few moments what a hellion I'd encountered. Sure, I was chuffed, thrilled, excited . . . couldn't believe my good fortune – as you say, it was a dream come true. She came at me like a panther, threw her arms around me and let

40

me have it with the lips. Norman, it was like kissing a sink plunger. Two minutes of this and she broke away, ripped open her dress and dropped it to the floor. Son, beneath that shapeless rag she was stark bollock naked – and what a body! Firm, round, and fully packed – knockers like bowling balls.'

'Getaway . . .' he gasped.

'In she came again, tearing at my trousers, feverish – nay, *demented* to get at it. Never have I known a bird so mad for it – nor will I ever meet her like again. In a thrice we were on the bed, going at it heaven's hard, and – believe this or believe it not – three hours later we were *still* at it!'

'Cor blimey O'Reilly . . . three *hours*!'

'She wanted it every which-way . . . on the bed, on the floor, kneeling down, standing up . . . Norman, she was insatiable . . . *insatiable*! Wanted more and more and more! Well, after three hours I was on my knees . . . shagged to a standstill. Enough, I begged, enough!'

'I should bleedin' think so.'

'But she wasn't having any of that mullarky. And that's when I realised she was round the twist, bats, cuckoo. Do it again, she cried, or I'll scream . . . tell them you forced me in here and raped me!'

'Oh, Christ, Albert . . .'

'And not only will you do it again *now*, she threatened, but you will stay in this house forever and do it to me every day and every night!'

'What . . . !'

'Straight up, Norman – as true as I'm standing here. Oh, right out of Tennessee Williams, this kid – she should've been locked up in the flaming attic – which is where, incidentally, she wanted to lock *me*!'

'Aw, go on . . .'

'No – true! She wanted to keep me up there as resident stud! Said she'd rigged out the attic with all mod. cons. and that I'd be very comfy up there . . .'

'Well, how did you finally get away?'

I tapped the side of my nose. 'Waited till she went down for tea with mum and the Rev. – then picked the lock and scarpered. Boy, I churned up gravel getting out of *that* nuthouse, I can tell you. And I didn't go back for the money, either.'

'Wow . . .' he gasped wonderingly. 'What an experience. Nothing like that ever happened to me. The only experience I had on a job was opening a bathroom door and finding the bird sitting on the loo . . . but she weighed twenty-two stone.'

'That's the breaks of the game, Norman. Personally I'd have preferred your experience.'

'Aw, go on,' he grinned. 'It must have been great for the first three hours, Albert.'

I shook my head. 'Unbelievable. Now – do you think we might do a little work? It is, after all, almost five o'clock . . .'

'Oh, yers, sorry, Albert . . . got quite carried away . . .'

'Yoo hoo!' called a voice from the hall below.

I stuck my head down through the hole, finding Mrs. P. on the bottom stair.

'Fancy a cup of tea, you two?'

'You just saved two lives,' I told her. 'Thanks very much.'

'Be right up.'

I got down the ladder to meet her. A minute later she arrived with a tray. She was still wearing the blouse over the bikini.

'You must be baked up there in the attic,' she said.

'Done to a turn. How about you?'

'Finished for the day. I'm now going to have a nice soak in the bath.'

'Sounds terrific. I could do with one myself.'

The same one!

'Yes, I'm sure. You must be exhausted, poor things.'

I took the tray from her. 'We'll be finishing soon. The ladder's ready to go in now. We'll do the flooring in the morning.'

'Ooh, the ladder's nearly finished! I'm dying to see it.'

'Well, you pop in and have your bath, and when you come out I'll be able to demonstrate it to you.'

'Ooh, super!'

She entered the bedroom and almost closed the door. Moments later I heard a swish of clothing, then she started humming to herself and I knew she was standing in the nude, admiring herself in the mirror. Birds always sing when they're naked.

Boy, what I'd have given to get an eye to the keyhole, but I daren't risk it. Instead, I climbed back into the loft and we had our tea.

42

A couple of minutes later she came out of the bedroom, dressed in a blue silk housecoat, her blonde hair piled up in a top-knot, and she headed for the bathroom. Soon water was gushing into the bath, then the heady aroma of exotic bath-oil reached our nostrils, causing Norman's eyes to cross.

'Oh, mate . . .' he groaned. 'Just imagine her slipping starkers into those bubbles.'

'Norman – to ladder.'

The installation of the ladder, now that the complex framework was done, was a simple matter, and as we'd finished long before she was due out of the bathroom I sent Norman to wait in the van. I wanted La Pinkerton to myself for a few minutes to find out what she had in mind.

So, when she did finally emerge, hot and bothered from the steamy bathroom and smelling like heaven itself, I was sitting on a lower rung of the ladder, waiting for her.

'Phew . . . !' she laughed, fanning her face with her hand. 'That feels better.'

'It sure smells terrific. I'm afraid it was all too much for Norman, he's gone to sit in the van. Perfume has that effect on him, you know.'

'Ah ha,' she nodded, picking up the cue. 'But I suppose you're hardened to it . . . through experience?'

'That would be telling, now, wouldn't it.'

'Oh, a girl doesn't need telling about such things,' she smiled, her eyes sexing up again. 'It shows.'

The realisation that we were alone now fully struck me, and the intimacy of the moment started my heart thumping something awful. Just me and this lovely bird – who was giving me the eyes – alone in the house, standing close to each other, right outside her bedroom door. Surely she was just as aware of it? She must *know* I fancied her like mad and was shaking inside at the sight of her?

Was she waiting for me to make a move? Was she standing there just aching to be swept into the bedroom and thrown on the bed? Dare I risk so much as touching her?

What a dilemma.

What if I *did* get hold of her, try to kiss her . . . and she began screaming the house down? I'd be arrested, finished, out of business.

Then again, what if I didn't and she was yearning for it? What a shocking waste.

'So – you've finished,' she said happily. 'It looks terrific. May I try it?'

'But certainly. Let me show you how it works.'

I slid up the lower section of the aluminium ladder, then gave the whole thing a push. Smooth as silk it folded up into the loft and the hatch cover closed with a quiet whooosh.

'Beautiful!' she exclaimed. 'Oh, that's just lovely. Now, how do I get it down?'

I brandished the short tubular rod with a hook in the end. 'Just reach up and hook this in the eyelet . . . and pull down like this.'

Down came the hatch cover and, with it, the ladder.

'Ingenious!' she enthused. 'Oh, I must have a go at that.'

She did . . . twice . . . three times.

'Albert, it's so clever! May I climb up the ladder?'

'Of course!'

I released the lower section and slid it to the floor. She got a muled foot on the first tread and gingerly began to climb. 'Ooh, it's a bit wobbly . . .'

It wasn't really, but birds say these things.

'Don't worry, I'm right behind you, I won't let you fall.'

Making a full five-course – and quite unnecessary – meal of it, like she was tackling Ben Nevis instead of a ten-rung ladder, she struggled to the top and stuck her head through the hole.

'Wonderful,' she said. 'It's so much easier now.'

'You'll be running up and down all day long, I can see.'

'Wonderful,' she repeated, and started her descent. 'Oh, I do hate ladders . . .'

'Fear not – Garth is right behind you.'

'It's a great comfort,' she grinned. Then, two rungs later, 'OOOPS! Hold me . . . !'

Now, whether she genuinely slipped or whether it was a beautifully contrived act, I am not prepared to swear, but instinctively my hands shot around her waist, and at that moment she turned and fell hard against me, simultaneously flinging her arms round my neck for protection.

Woomf! Our bodies collided, my arms tightened around her . . . and there we hung, suspended, staring into each other's

44

eyes, the realisation of our intimate juxtaposition boffing us good and proper.

In the next moment I knew it had all been sneakily contrived. Her eyes smoked up and her mouth curved in a delicious grin. 'Hi . . .' she whispered huskily.

Now that the green light was flashing, Shifty, though momentarily overwhelmed and unable to believe his luck, was not backward at coming forward.

'Hi, yourself,' I grinned, my voice broken and croaky and my heart thundering in my chest. Just for fun I kissed her on the nose.

'That's naughty,' she breathed breathlessly.

'Then how about this?'

This time I went for her mouth . . . and it was more than ready. With a groan she thrust hard into me, drove her hot mouth into mine, shot her tongue between my lips and filled my mouth with it.

Up rose the mighty Rodney, stiff as a sail boom, and at his impertinent thrust she murmured a feverish 'Ohhhhhhh!' and crashed her belly into him. 'Ohhh, Albert . . .'

For a good three minutes we made a mess of each other, then, finally, flushed and breathless, she broke away, wild-eyed and jubilant. 'Wow . . . !' she gasped. 'You really come on strong!'

'You're not so . . . fragile yourself,' I panted.

She brushed hair from her face and heaved a steadying breath, gulped a couple of times, then gave a light-hearted shrug. 'So . . . ?'

'So I get rid of Norman. He can drive the van home, I'll walk.'

'You'll be seen.'

'Not in the dark.'

Her eyes danced wickedly. 'Albert, it does not get dark until ten o'clock.'

'I'll still walk.'

'You . . .' she said, prodding me on the nose, '. . . are evil. Go on – get rid of Norman.'

Floating in a miasma of unreality I bounded down the stairs and out to the van, unable to control the ear-to-ear grin as I approached Norman. 'Go on – scarper.'

'Eh?'

'I said scarper! Go home, get lost, I'll see you later.'

Dawning realisation turned his gape into a different kind of gape. 'You're staying!'

'In a word – yes. I trust it satisfies you to know you were right.'

'No kiddin'! Hey, Albert . . . she *has* got the hots for you!'

'More like the scalds. Now, go on, push off, I should be home about eleven, but don't hold your breath waiting.'

'What about her old man?'

I shrugged. 'Not a word. I don't reckon there is one. Either that or he's taking a cruise up the Congo.'

'You lucky stiff.'

'That's about the size of it. Give you the scam later.'

'Promise?'

'Not likely, you'd die of excitement.'

'I'll be thinking about you, Albert,' he said, starting the engine. 'Cor, it actually happened. Of all the lucky baskets . . .'

'Good*bye*, Norman.'

I was back up the drive before he was into second gear.

I closed the door and quickly climbed the stairs, the old tumult beginning inside my chest again. Hesitantly I went along the landing, wondering where she was, then she called out softly from the bedroom. 'Albert . . . in here.'

I went in and found her sitting at her dressing table, brushing out her hair. She flashed me a grin in the mirror, then, quite calmly, said, 'Would you *like* that bath?'

'I certainly would.'

She waved the brush. 'Help yourself.'

'Okay . . .'

I lay in deep suds, grinning to myself and pondering on the wonders of life. Who, at eight o'clock this morning, would have imagined that nine hours later I'd be wallowing in Pinkerton's bath? At eight this morning I didn't even know Pinkerton existed!

I sure as hell did now, though.

Who was she? What – apart from a scrumptious and sexually ravenous bird – was she?

Yours is not to reason why, Albert . . . yours is to thank your lucky stars and get stuck in, 'cause that's what the lady wants.

I nipped out of the bath and towelled off, once again stricken with the inner trembles at the prospect of what was in the offing. And *still* I couldn't believe my luck.

Dressed again, I ventured back along the landing, approached her bedroom, found the door almost closed and the room beyond almost in darkness, the curtains drawn.

'Come in,' she said softly.

I pushed open the door, popped my head in, found her lying on the top of the bed, still in her robe.

'Close the door.'

I closed it. Now she was little more than a vague shape on the bed. She patted the counterpane. 'Come and sit down.'

I sat close to her, my heart-beat rocking my body.

'It's Vickie, by the way.'

'Vickie . . .'

She smiled. 'I'm sure you were wondering what to call me. "Mrs. Pinkerton" sounds ridiculously formal in the circumstances.'

'Yes,' I laughed, wondering who was going to make the first move.

She did.

Her hands went to the sash of her gown and with slow deliberation she unfastened it, laid it aside, then, with the same easy self-assurance, opened the gown wide, revealing her nakedness.

Bombs away.

I got to my feet, whipped off the shirt, dropped the jeans, and was in beside her in a flash. Her arms shot out and grabbed me, hauled me on top of her, her legs spreading wide to take me.

'Oh, Albert . . .' she whispered, her voice tremulous, her urgent need evident in her panting breath and writhing hips. 'Albert, I want it fast and hard . . . now . . . *now*!'

Boom boom!

I took a sighter on her and drove in Rodders all the way home, evoking an ecstatic gasp from her as he struck the buffers.

'My God, you're en*ormous* . . . ! Oh, Albert . . . Albert . . . !'

Then she was away . . . a-hump-tee-hump-tee-hump-tee-dump, legs like an iron hoop locked round my waist for maximum penetration, driving me home with cries and gasps and grunts and moans, then . . . 'Albert, I'm *coming* . . . ! Oh, I'm . . . OHHHH! . . . EEEHH! . . . OOOOH! . . . AAAAHHH! . . . OHHHHHHHHHH!'

She hit a beaut but kept right on going, mouth gaping, eyes clamped tight, her face a grimace of sweet agony, fingers clawing the meat from my shoulders.

'Ohhhh . . . Ohhhhh . . . Ohhhhhh . . . OHHHHHHHHH!!'

Blimey she was into another.

'Go . . . ! Go . . . ! GO . . . !!' she cried, bucking harder than ever, the bedsprings squeaking like a symphony orchestra tuning up. 'Oh, Albert . . . Albert! Hit me . . . hit me!'

'Wo-o-o-o-o-o-OOOW!' I bellowed.

Ker . . . POW!

The Kariba Dam exploded into fragments.

'YAAAAHHHH!' she cried, sneaking another while no one was looking. 'Ohhh . . . ohhh . . . Oh, my God . . .'

Collapse.

Hee haw . . . hee haw . . . we lay there inflating and deflating like a couple of anaesthetist's balloons, gradually calming . . . calming, finally coming to rest, speechless, entirely blasted.

'*Oh* . . .' she groaned, heaving a huge, satisfied sigh which lifted me high and lowered me gently. 'That was . . .' She shook her head and rumbled a chuckle.

'It sure was,' I grinned. 'Am I too heavy for you?'

'Stay right where you are.'

She heaved another relish-filled sigh and exhaled it in a sensuous moan.

'Sounds like you needed that,' I said.

She nodded. 'I *needed* it.'

'Awfully glad I was on hand.'

She gave me a hug. 'I need a cigarette.'

'I'll get them.'

We sat side-by-side, propped up against the padded head-board, the room still in semi-darkness though light enough to see each other. There was no embarrassment, no shyness. I felt I'd known her for ever.

'Well, that *was* a surprise,' I grinned. 'Not *quite* what I expected when I arrived this morning.'

'I did.'

I looked at her.

She nodded. 'As soon as I opened the door to you I knew I was going to have you.'

'Well, I'll be damned.'

'I've suffered agonies of waiting all day. I was thinking about how you'd be while I was lying out there in the sun. I got *terribly* horny, you've no idea.'

I exploded a laugh. 'And I thought only men had such thoughts. Well, now that you've confessed, I can reveal I felt the same way about you, too.'

'I know. I could tell the way you were looking at me. I knew it would happen, that's what made the waiting unbearable. I had it in mind to seduce you at lunchtime, but your friend Norman was in the way.'

'Well, I'll be . . . If I'd known that I'd have sacked him as soon as we got here.'

'Will you tell him?'

'No, of course not. He may suspect, but I'll spin him a yarn. If you like, I'll come alone tomorrow, there's only the flooring to put in.'

'Yes . . .' she said quietly, 'come by yourself tomorrow,' and I could tell from the tone of her voice she was coming to the boil again.

She stubbed out her cigarette, took mine from between my fingers and ground it out in the ashtray, placed the ashtray on her bedside table, then slid down in the bed. 'Come here . . .' she whispered, reaching for me. 'There's something about you I find curiously irresistible.'

'Oh . . . ?' I gulped. 'What is it – my charm, personality, genius I.Q.?'

'Don't . . . be ridiculous.'

'Ooops! That's very forward of you.'

'You keep out of it . . . this is between him and me.'

*   *   *

'Albert . . . ?'

'Yes, love?'

'Did anybody ever tell you you were pretty damn good at this?'

'No.'

'Well, you're being told now.'

'Thank you.'

'Your talents are wasted installing loft-ladders, you could be making a fortune on this estate. At ten pounds per frustrated housewife, you'd be a millionaire in a year.'

'No kidding,' I laughed. 'Are there so many of them?'

'If you came to one of our parties you'd think so. To hear the girls talk there's not one who gets it to her satisfaction.'

'And why's that, d'you suppose?'

She shrugged. 'Different reasons, but mainly a lack of romance. Most of them have been married for a few years, have kids, their husbands are out all day and life has settled in a great yawning rut of washing, ironing, shopping, cooking and gardening. Their husbands come home tired, expect their meal to be on the table, watch a bit of tellie, then go to bed. Mostly, sex had become mechanical – if they do it at all. There are an awful lot of frustrated women in Belview. I reckon you could do them a great service.'

'Sounds promising,' I grinned. 'And what's your particular problem?'

'Mine . . .' she sighed, 'is a husband who is currently dedicated to searching for his lost youth. He's older than I am – thirty-two. We've been married five years. Things were fine until a year ago when he suddenly became aware that he was losing his hair, which triggered off a panic to stay young. He bought a motor bike – he had one when he was seventeen and used to flash around with a pal, impressing the girls – and he now spends most of his spare time doing the same thing. He's touring Devon with a buddy at the moment – "doing his own thing".'

'Oh, dear.'

'Yeah. So what the hell – I'm doing mine,' she smiled and cuddled closer. 'You saved my sanity.'

'You don't have sex with him?'

'Once in a blue moon. He has to save it for the dollies. Too much with me would rock his confidence out there.'

'Do you think he'll grow out of it?'

'I'm beginning not to care. And at this very moment I do not care at all.'

She bent and kissed my nipple. 'You're quite a fella. I think

50

I'll take you to Majorca with me.'

'You're not going with your husband?'

'No – I'm going solo, he suggested it. It was Devon for him and Majorca for me.'

'You'll have a ball.'

'I damn-well intend to. I've held out for a year but now you've broken my duck and I like it. I'm going to spread my wings and fly . . . life's too short.'

'Amen to that. So. – Belview is one seething mass of frustration?'

'And intrigue. You wouldn't be*lieve* the things that go on here . . . wife-swapping, orgies, blue-film shows . . .'

'You're kidding! In *Putney*!'

'Sure,' she laughed. 'People are people wherever. Boy, you ought to come to one of our parties . . .'

'I'd love to.'

'Right – when I get back I'll invite you. You won't *be* with me, but I'll get you an invite. It'll open your eyes. Putney will never be the same again.'

'Neither will I, by the sound of things.'

'Oh, you'll go down a treat with the girls. A new male face – especially a handsome one – causes more excitement than a bit of juicy gossip. You'll be the toast of the estate. Wouldn't surprise me if you picked up an *awful* lot of work here. You'll make a fortune.'

'That sounds very promising. I'll have to cut you in for ten percent as my agent.'

She grinned and shook her head. 'Not ten percent, Albert . . . *I* know what I want as payment.'

'Oh – what's that?' I asked ridiculously.

It was almost midnight by the time she got through telling me and by then she'd collected a damn-sight more than ten percent.

She'd collected the lot!

CHAPTER THREE

It was after one o'clock when I climbed out of the taxi and managed to locate the keyhole. Opening the front door, I slipped into the Kranki hallway, removed my shoes, and tip-toed across the lino towards the stairs. I never made them. With an excited yip, a long, low brown torpedo shot out of the shadows and launched a rape attack on my right ankle.

'Aw, Fritz . . .' I groaned. 'Come off it, mate . . . just the thought of it'll kill me.'

I picked him up, sat down heavily on the stairs and gave him a cuddle.

'Yes, I know, I know, and I think it's a rotten shame. We humans can go out and find it, but you've got to wait for any-thing that comes along. Between you and me, though, cock, I couldn't fancy the umbrella stand no matter how rough things got. Now, off you go and take a nice cold shower – and get your mind on more worthwhile things – like biting Mr. Philby.'

I gave him a pat on the bum and sent him on his way, but he wasn't having any. He turned to face me and let go a deafening yap of insolent defiance.

'Ssssshh!' I hissed. 'Go on – piss off!'

Yap!

'You'll wake the bleeding house up!'

Yap! Yap!

That did it.

A door in the lower hall opened. I turned to flee but had only made five stairs when an imperative 'Pssssstt!' stopped me in my tracks.

Gingerly, expecting an irate Frau Kranki, I turned back, but encountered the mortifying sight of Dillys in curlers and an almost see-through nightie. My word, she *was* a big girl.

'What have you been up to?' she whispered, starting up the stairs, the excitement in her eye at having got me alone at last horrifyingly evident.

'Dillys . . . go back!'

'Ha!'

I turned and scrambled up to the first landing, peered back . . . Christ, she was still coming!

'Go back!' I hoarsed, but still she came.

There was nothing else to do but run.

Shattered, I fell into my room and closed the door, leaned against it, gasping for breath. She wouldn't follow . . . wouldn't *dare* follow, not all this way up.

Baff!

I shot across the room, propelled by the door, and by the time I'd recovered she was inside, door closed.

'Dillys, this is madness!'

'I told you I'd do it,' she beamed. 'There's nothing to worry about, my mother's snoring her head off.'

'Aw, Dillys, no . . . I'm all in, love. I've had a very hard day.'

Her eyes narrowed. 'Yers – so Norman told me.'

'Eh? What did he tell you?'

'About that blonde woman you're working for.'

I frowned. 'Well, he had no right to . . .'

She grinned despicably. 'He had no choice – I twisted his arm until he told me what you were up to. I knew you were up to something when he came home alone.'

'It's none of your business. Besides . . . I wasn't "up to" anything. It so happens she had a couple of little extra jobs she wanted doing and . . .'

'Huh – I'll bet! Like her for a start.'

'Dillys, you have an *exceed*ingly low mind.'

'Yers – haven't I?'

And on that she tripped across the floor and plonked down on the bed. 'Talk to me.'

'I shall do no such thing,' I said, collecting my soap, towel and toothbrush. 'I am nipping down for a quick bath, and upon my return I expect to find you gone. No – better still – you'll leave with me now.'

'Aw, Albert . . .'

'Come!'

Pouting magnificently, she dragged herself off the bed and slouched through the door. I followed her out and down the first flight of stairs.

'Goodnight, Dillys,' I whispered.

'You don't like me.'

'I do – but in less suicidal surroundings. See you in the morning.'

I gave her a finger wave and ducked into the bathroom, at last able to breathe a sigh of relief.

Drawing a deep, hot soak, I steeped myself to the neck and allowed my mind to range over the events of the afternoon. What a turn-up. Fancy it all coming to fruition like that. And what a future! Even supposing that Pinkerton was overstating the case, there had to be at least a dozen frustrated females to whom I could offer understanding and consolation – with a job thrown in!

Yes, the future did indeed look bright.

Brimming over with high spirits, I nipped out of the bath and within five minutes was in bed, naked of course – I always sleep in the nod – feeling all rosy, relaxed and ready for the high dive.

Goodnight, Pinky, love, see you in the morning. Sleep tight, get your batteries charged up . . . and see what the angels bring you.

Zonk! I was asleep.

Probably because I'd gone to sleep with her on my mind, I was soon dreaming about her. I was lying on her bed when she came into the room, starkers, and lay down beside me, the dream incredibly real because I experienced the sensation of the bed tilting.

'Albert . . . ?' she mewed.

'Yes, love?'

'I want you.'

'Yes, love.'

Her hand strayed to my thigh and ran up it, then pounced on Rodney, bringing him up with a rush. By God, the dream *was* real! Incredible sensation. I mean, her hand was really *there*!

I came out of sleep, playing with myself.

Eh?

No, I wasn't – both hands were on my chest!

Then who . . . ?

'He's *gorgeous*,' husked Dillys, her hot breath on my cheek. I shot up, heart thundering. 'Dillys . . . !'

'Shut up and lie down,' she commanded, smashing me back

into the pillows with a forearm chop. 'Don't pretend you didn't know I was doing it.'

'I . . . I was asleep!'

'*No*body sleeps through this, Albert. Oh, Albert, please stop pretending and put your mind to it. I mean, I'm here now, so you may as well enjoy it.'

Well, she certainly had a point.

'That's better,' she cooed, feeling me relax. 'I knew you'd see sense. Just think of all the nights we've wasted. Still, better late than never. There, isn't that nice, Albert?'

'L . . . lovely,' I gulped.

It was, too. She had the softest, gentlest hands.

'I've dreamed about doing this to you, Albert. Night after night I lie in my lonely bed and imagine myself climbing the stairs, entering your room while you're asleep, climbing into your bed . . . and doing this. And now it's all come true.'

'I've had one or two similar thoughts about you, too, Dillys.'

'Have you, Albert? What kind of thoughts?'

'I'd better not tell you, you might run screaming down the stairs.'

'Fat chance,' she chuckled. '*Anything* you want to do is fine by me.'

Oh, boy.

I couldn't believe my luck! Blimey, months and months of enforced celibacy up there in my rat cage, then – wham! suddenly more than I could cope with. Well, not *more*, but certainly as much as I could comfortably handle.

'Dillys, you'd . . . better stop doing that or I shall not be responsible for the consequences.'

She gave an evil chuckle. 'Why, what will happen, Albert?'

'Don't be ridiculous.'

'Albert . . . ?'

'Yes, Dilly?'

'I've got a book.'

'What sort of book?'

'A book of sex instruction. I bought it weeks ago and I've been studying it.'

I gulped. 'You have?'

'I didn't realise there were so many ways of doing it . . . or so many lovely things to do. Albert . . . ?'

'Yes, Dillys.'

'I . . . I'd like to try them all with you . . . every one of them. Could I?'

'Well, I . . .' I gave a cough. Why the hell not! 'Sure,' I grinned, 'why not?'

'Oh, you are kind. There's . . . just one more thing, Albert . . .'

'What's that, love?'

'Do you mind if we have just a little light on? I don't like doing it in the dark.'

'No, go ahead. I don't like the dark myself.'

Click!

The darkness vanished in the glow of an unfamiliar light-source, a subdued and pleasant loom which seemed to emanate from the floor by the side of the bed.

'What . . . where did that come from?' I frowned.

'I brought my torch up,' she grinned. 'The book was very insistent on the lighting being right.'

I saw now that she'd got rid of the curlers and was still wearing the almost see-through nightie. The book was right – in this light she looked terrific.

Beaming happily, she knelt up at my side, caught hold of the hem of the nightie and whipped it over her head; the sight of her voluptuous body, sturdy thighs and huge, fleshy breasts, causing excitement to thunder through me.

'Wow . . .' I gasped.

'Do I please you, Albert?'

She didn't wait for an answer, but fell forward on me and smothered me with eager flesh, covering my chest with a hail of teasing kisses and quickly working down to my stomach.

'One . . . thing the . . . book . . . emphasised . . .' she murmured between kisses, '. . . was that as much . . . as anything else . . . a man enjoys . . . THIS!'

YaaaHOOOOO!

Into her succulent mouth popped Rodders and I went through the roof.

By gum, she must have worked overtime on that book – she knew it chapter and verse, sentence and full stop – by heart. She gave me a right old going over.

'Dillys . . . Dillys . . . stop . . . stop!'

56

'Okay – we'll try something else.'

Up she rose, kneeling high above me, then whipped one leg across me, took a sighter on Rodney and down she plunged.

'Ohhhh . . . Albert!' she gasped, shaking her fists at the ceiling. 'It's *gor*geous! They said it was and it is! It is!'

'Ssssshhh!' I chuckled. 'You'll wake the house up!'

'I don't care . . . I don't *care*! Ohhhh . . . ! Ohh, boy . . . ohhhh, this is fan*tas*tic!'

Yap!

Her eyes flew wide – with horror. Mine were already there. Yap! Yap! went Fritz again – RIGHT OUTSIDE MY DOOR!

Dillys gasped. 'Oh . . . NO!'

'Oh, my God . . . Quick! Shut him up! Get him in!'

She was off like a rocket.

YAP! YAP! YAP! YAP! YAP!

'Fritz – shut up!'

She jerked open the door.

YAP! YAP! YAP!

'Come here, you stupid . . .'

She made a grab for him but he shot back, enjoying the game.

YAP! YAP YAPPITY-YAP! YAP! . . . YAP! YAP!

A door opened on a lower landing. 'Vat iss goink on up zer?' demanded Von Brik's stertorian bellow. 'Vat iss Fritz doink up zer?'

'Christ . . . !' gasped the naked Dillys, and shot back into the room. 'What are we going to do!'

I was out of bed in a trice, bemused, befuddled, dumb with funk. 'I . . . er . . . erm . . . oh . . . well, get your nightie on for a *start*!'

She grabbed for it, dropped it, picked it up, got it on back-to-front, whipped it off, got it on right, all the time groaning pitifully, 'What are we going to *do*!'

'Keep calm . . . keep calm!' I said, leaping over the bed and plucking my dressing gown out of the wardrobe. 'Nobody knows you're up here.'

'Bloody Fritz does!'

YAP! YAP! YAP! he barked, as though confirming the fact.

57

'*I'll* deal with Fritz!' I declared boldly, opening the door. 'EEK!' I squeaked, and closed it a damn-sight faster.

'What is it?' she gasped.

'Your mother! Quick – under the bed!'

'You must be joking!'

'In the wardrobe, then!'

She shot across the room, opened the door, tried to get in. 'I . . . can't!'

'You've got to!'

I ran to help her, squeezed her in, pushed, shoved, finally got the door closed.

'I'm suffocating!'

'Then hold your breath!'

'Vat iss goink on up here?' demanded Frau Kranki.

A babble of voices answered her. Christ, the entire household was on the top floor!

I nipped across and opened the door, putting on a just-woken-up act. 'What's . . . going on . . .'

Blimey, they were all there – all, that is, except Dillys!

YAP! YAP! YAP! barked Fritz, now secure in Herr Von Brik's arms.

'Vy iss he barkink?' demanded Frau Kranki. 'Vy iss he up here? He never koms up here.'

'I don't know,' replied Von Brik, narrowing his eyes in my direction. 'But I sink he smells a rat!'

'Zer are no rats in my house!' protested Frau Kranki.

'Not *zat* kind of rat,' insisted Von Brik, his eyes now slits of cruel suspicion. 'He was barkink at Herr Shifty's door – und perhaps ve should be askink ourselves vy!'

'My door!' I gasped, outraged. 'Now, look here Von Brik . . .'

'Perhaps . . .' continued Von Brik with hellish satisfaction, 'zer iss somesink in Herr Shifty's room zat should *not* be zer?'

'Somesink like what?' demanded Frau Kranki, her own eyes emulating Von Brik's.

'I dunno,' shrugged Von Brik. 'But obviously Fritz does. Vy don't ve let him find out?'

Oh, my sainted aunt. Once that little bastard set paw on the floor, he'd make a bee-line for the wardrobe and the game would be up! I decided, therefore, that the best form of defence was attack.

'Von Brik, I don't know what you're talking about. I've got nothing in my room that shouldn't be there and . . .'

YAP! YAP! YAP! went Fritz, which is dog for 'you're a flaming liar, Shifty.' No doubt he was getting his own back for that kick in the throat.

'Obviously Fritz does not agree,' sneered Von Brik glee-fully, transparently getting *his* own back for the jokes at breakfast.

'But vat could he have in his room zat should not be zer?' asked Frau Kranki, now beginning to enjoy this interrogation.

Von Brik shrugged again. 'A . . . stranger maybe?'

Frau Kranki gasped. 'A . . . woman!'

The assembly exploded in a babble. Van Gogh, Harriet Bloom, Bennie, Harry, Peter and Norman leaping to my defence, Dan Philby piling into the attack.

'Precisely the sort of immorality one would expect!' he charged.

'Aw, belt up, Philby,' roared Harriet.

'Take the dog downstairs,' put in Bennie. 'I've gotta get some sleep.'

'The whole thing's a lot of nonsense,' protested Fred Van Gogh. 'Who knows what gets into a dog's mind?'

'Dogs do not bark at nossink at three o'clock in ze mornink!' challenged Von Brik.

YAP! YAP! YAP! agreed Fritz.

'See – he knows somesink! I say zer iss a stranger in zis house und must be exposed!'

'Mein Gott,' gasped Frau Kranki, slapping her forehead.

'You're out of your mind, Von Brik!' I shouted, backing towards my door, knowing he was going to loose the dogs of war any second now. 'How dare you . . .'

'I dare!' he cried triumphantly, and dropped Fritz to the floor.

I froze, shut my eyes, knowing the end had come. I heard Fritz's claws scratching at the lino, trying to get purchase, then the little swine would be in like a bullet and barking at the wardrobe. There would be a wail of protest from Frau Kranki as Dillys fell out into the room and then . . . my mind blanked off, protecting me from the nightmare that was to follow.

Thump!

But no . . . !

Fritz had not shot past me into the room! The sight of my right leg had proved too much for the randy little git and he was now pummelling away like there was no tomorrow!

The assembly burst into laughter. I opened my eyes and looked down, visually patting the little blighter on the head. Go to it, Fritz, old kid, it's all yours!

'Well, would you believe it,' grinned Harriet. 'He's in love with Albert! It was *Albert* he wanted!'

I bent down and picked Fritz up, and, right on cue, he showered my chin with licks.

'Elbert, I . . .' said Frau Kranki helplessly.

'Humph,' went Von Brik, glowering with disappointment, then smartly about-turned and clumped down the stairs.

'We'll make the wedding next week,' I said, handing Fritz to Frau Kranki.

Laughing, everybody dispersed.

'Elbert, I'm sorry . . .' muttered Frau Kranki. 'I should haf known you would never haf a woman in your room. I vill lock Fritz up in future so zat zis cannot happen again.'

YAP! protested Fritz, eyeing the wardrobe behind me.

'Shaddap!' snapped Frau Kranki. 'You I must take to za vet for bromide pills, you are over-sexed! Goodnight, Elbert.'

'Goodnight, Mrs. Kranki.'

She went down the stairs, leaving only Norman there, half-asleep and scratching his head. 'What a rum thing to happen, he's never done that before.'

'True love takes its time, Norman.'

He grinned. 'Fancy thinkin' you had a bird in your room. Chance'd be a fine thing, eh? Which reminds me – how did you get on with . . .'

I shook my head. 'No dice.' I heaved a disgruntled sigh. 'All talk and no action, son – just wanted to chat, that was all.'

'Ooh, what a disappointment. I could've sworn you were well-in there.'

'That's life,' I shrugged. 'Well, back to my lonely room . . .'

'Yeah,' he sighed. 'You can say that again. Goodnight, Albert . . .'

'Goodnight, son . . .'

'A-a-a-a-a-a . . . ccchhhoooooo!' Dillys let go a mother-and-father of a sneeze.

Norman's eyes popped. 'What . . . ?'

I levelled a finger at him. 'Not a word!'

A grin cleaved his face. 'You crafty . . . Albert, I want a raise.'

'Take tomorrow off instead.'

'Done!'

'Goodnight!'

'Goodnight!'

I nipped into my room and closed the door, ran to the wardrobe and yanked it open, finding Dillys in a state of apoplexy. She stumbled out and fell across the bed, gasping for breath, bosoms heaving.

'Lie still . . . I'll go and get you a drink of water.'

I shot down to the bathroom, filled a glass, and crept back up again, coming to a stunned halt as I slipped into the room. The light was off and the torch was on the floor again – and Dillys was lying on the bed stark naked.

'Dillys . . . you're mad!'

She gave a big sexy grin. 'We only got to page two in the manual, we can't stop now.'

I gulped, mortified by her determination. 'And . . . how many pages are there?'

'Four hundred and eighty seven.' She patted the bed at her side. 'Come . . .'

She wasn't kidding, either.

CHAPTER FOUR

Well, after all that excitement things settled down a bit. The
following day I nipped back to Pinkerton's pad and put the
floor (and a couple of other things) in for her and left her a
very happy woman. In return she promised, when she came
back from Majorca, to drum up a bit of business for me around
the estate, so I drove away a very happy fella.

The following day I picked up a painting and decorating job
in Fulham for a nice old girl who'd just collected on an in-
surance policy and who was so over-joyed that she'd out-lived
the premiums, she bought a bottle of gin and got blind drunk
while we were putting up the wall-paper.

Thursday was quiet, so Norman and I went to Lord's to see
the M.C.C. get beaten by 114 wickets and 9,000 runs by the
West Indians.

Friday we spent doing a bit of gardening for a woman in
Richmond.

And then came Saturday.

Funny how you know certain days are doom-laden the
moment you open your eyes, isn't it?

Thump! went my alarm clock.

'Eight o'clock, Albert!'

'Weather report, Norman?'

'It's pissing darn!'

My spirits plummeted. Well, I suppose it was to be expected. Four consecutive fine days *was* something of a miracle.

I lumbered out of bed and flung back the curtains. One
thing about Norman, he is not given to exaggeration. It was
pissing down. The sky was as black as a miner's earhole and
thunder rumbled through the heavens.

Collecting my bins from the dresser, I gave the landscape a
cursory sweep, locating three spadgers having a watery frolic in
the gutter of 76 and a half-drowned starling sheltering on a
window-sill. Then on to Esme Pickersgill's window just in time
to catch her flinging back the drapes.

Ah, she looked a treat this morning in a diaphonous black

62

creation, Empire style, which emphasised, quite unnecessarily, the proud burgeon of her sensational knockers.

Three steps back and off it came. My blood came to the boil for the day. With bated breath I watched her execute the Stork position, then the Plough, and by the time she got round to standing on her head I had a raging hard-on that would've frightened even Pinkerton . . . almost.

Thus randied-up for the day, I stowed away the binocs, attired myself in my dressing gown and collected my shaving gear, my thoughts not unsurprisingly turning to the lovely Dillys and to the prospect of luring her to my lair again. Ever since that near-fateful night she had chosen to play it cool, believing, as I believed, that Von Brik's radar was still directed towards my room and to my comings and goings. She had, therefore, backed off a touch in order to allay his suspicions, with the direct consequence that I now fancied her more than ever.

Still – time, as they say, healed all, and it would not be long before we could resume our progress through her sex manual, a process which promised to be an extremely protracted affair since, despite whole-hearted dedication on that first night we were still only on page three!

'Finished, Albert!' announced Norman.

I opened the door, descended the stairs, and was about to enter the bathroom when none other than the adorable Dillys rounded the turn on the lower landing and gasped, 'Ahhhh! I want you!'

I cast a furtive glance around. 'Dillys! In broad daylight!'

Grinning, she came up the rest of the way and made a sneaky attack inside my gown. 'I've been pining for him!' she whispered, grabbing hold of Rodders. 'Oh, Albert, I need him!'

'Dillys, we can't . . . ! Von Brik . . .'

'I know, I know . . . give it a few more days.'

'Well, what are you doing up here!'

'Telephone . . . there's a call for you. Couldn't miss the opportunity. Oh, dear . . . he's growing!'

'I *know* he's . . .'

She stifled a giggle. 'Come on, hide it with your towel.'

Bent almost double, I followed her down to the hall, Dillys killing herself laughing.

'Sounds like a kid,' she said, indicating the telephone. 'Let me know if it's a baby-sitting job, I'll come round and sit with you . . .'

'Dillys!' bellowed Frau Kranki from the kitchen.

'Coming, mother!'

She blew me a kiss and disappeared. I picked up the phone. 'Hello?'

'Is that Albert as in "Let Albert Do It"?' enquired a beautifully modulated child's voice.

'Yes,' I frowned. 'Who's this?'

'I . . .' he announced superiorly, 'am Master Geoffrey Hyde-Wallace . . . and I am speaking on behalf of my grandfather, Colonel St. John Hyde-Wallace.'

'Really,' I grinned, tickled by the tone of outrageous authority. 'And what can I do for you, Master Hyde-Wallace?'

'My grandfather saw your advertisement in the local paper and asked me to call to see if you would undertake a job of attic clearance for him.'

'Attic clearance? Yes, we do that sort of work. When does he want it done?'

'As soon as possible – preferably today. Could you come today?'

'Yes, we could. What's the address?'

'It's a very large house on Victoria Drive . . . it's called Monks Haunt.'

'Sounds fun,' I grinned, but he wasn't having any.

'Do you know where Victoria Drive is?'

'Yes – just off Wimbledon Common. And what time would he like us to be there?'

'As soon as possible, he has to go out at eleven o'clock.'

'All right – we'll be there at ten.'

'He'll be much obliged,' he announced and rang off.

Chuckling, I replaced the receiver. You've got to hand it to the toffs, they do have bags of style, buckets of confidence. No wonder they own ninety-five percent of the world.

I tottered upstairs to break the news to Norman, knowing he'd be pleased with an indoor job on a lousy day like this.

'Monk's Haunt?' he frowned. 'Blimey, that sounds cheerful.

One of them ninety-roomed mausoleums, by the sound of things.'

'Undoubtedly – but dry, Norman.'

'Much money in it?'

'The child's tone did not allow for the discussion of remuneration. He made it perfectly clear they were stretching a point by allowing us to do the job.'

'Sounds a right snobby little sod to me.'

'It's not his fault, Norman – it's his upbringing. He is taught at prep-school that the sun shines only on the Hyde-Wallaces of the world, and that the Shiftys and the Normans are to be approached as one would a leper – sympathetically but most definitely from a distance.'

'Like I say – a right snobby little sod.'

'Crudely vernacular,' I nodded, 'but absolutely spot on. Come – let us to breakfast and *really* make it a lousy day.'

The dining room was a-buzz with customary bonhomie. Fred Van Gogh was in the throes of a summer cold and Dan Philby had cut his throat shaving, though not deeply enough by far. Harry and Peter appeared to have had a tiff and Harriet Bloom had just laddered her tights on the chair-leg. Ernst Von Brik was in his usual silent, watchful mood, still smarting from defeat and fretful for revenge, and only Bennie appeared to be in good spirits.

'Kill the cornflakes, Dillys,' I told her. 'I'll just have the afters. Morning, Bennie.'

'Watcha, cock, how's business?'

'On the up and up. Got an attic clearance this morning – Colonel St. John Hyde-Wallace. Should be good for a laugh. Probably a roomful of shrunken heads and stuffed tigers. How're things with you?'

'I have been seriously contemplating a change of profession. I believe my particular talents are being wasted on the 48 route.'

'Oh – a change to what?'

'Gigolo,' he said, and Von Brik spluttered in his coffee. 'Reckon I could do myself a bit of good on those cruise ships around the Caribbean . . . all those rich birds looking for a bit of indigenous romance. I'll have to tune up my bongos and give it a whirl.'

Von Brik's fork hit the plate. 'Really! Iss the conversation at zis table forever to be confined to ze gutter! I find it puerile, imbecilic und repulsive!'

'You said that yesterday,' Bennie reminded him.

'Bah!' Von Brik exploded, springing to his feet. 'In future I shall take my meals in mein room!'

'Aw, siddown,' said Harriet. 'The boys are only having a bit of fun. And you must admit it takes your mind off the food.'

'Food?' enquired Dillys, steaming in to place a plate before me. 'What's that?'

'And what's that!' I asked, peering at the plate.

'Guess.'

'Er . . . scrambled eggs?'

'Guess again.'

'Omelette?'

'Ha!'

'Well, give me a clue – is it anyone we *know*?'

'I refuse to answer on the grounds that it might incriminate my mother.'

'I'll just have coffee.'

She slapped her forehead. 'Is there no *end* to this man's courage.'

Shatter! went Norman's toast, right on cue, this time into Philby's coffee.

Now Philby threw down his fork. 'I've had enough!'

'Don't blame you, Philby,' I said. 'You should try the haddock for a change.'

'In future I shall take my meals in *my* room, too!' he fumed, thrusting back his chair and leaping to his feet, little realising he had inadvertently tucked the table cloth into his trousers.

Crash! Clatter! Tinkle! Onto the floor shot Norman's plate, cup and cutlery.

'Aw, heck, Mister Philby, I was enjoying that.'

'Ohhh . . . shut up!' cried Philby and stormed from the room, hastily followed by Von Brik.

'Vot iss goink *on* in ziss crazy house!' demanded Frau Kranki through the hatch.

'Mister Philby took exception to his omelette,' I told her. 'He threw it on the floor. Personally speaking, if there's any

66

more of this puerile, imbecilic and repulsive behaviour I shall be forced to take my meals in my room.'

'Omelette?' she frowned. 'But he had fish pie!'

'No wonder he was furious.' I winked at Norman. 'Come on, we've got work to do.'

'On an empty stomach!'

'Quit while you're ahead,' muttered Dillys. 'Here – nibble on this.'

'A dog biscuit!'

'Don't knock it – think what they do for Fritz.'

'Come on,' I said, steering him out of the door. 'And keep your eyes off that umbrella stand.'

*   *   *

It was still bucketing down when we turned into Victoria Drive, the leaden darkness of the sky glooming up the scene a treat and making the big old houses more uninviting than ever.

Monks Haunt was a beaut – four storeys-above-garden of mouldering antiquity, surrounded by a garden of jungle-dense rhododendrons and dripping hydrangeas, and as we drove through the pillared gate-way and up the gravel drive, I was seized with the most urgent desire to swing the van round hard and drive right out again.

'Oh, blimey,' muttered Norman, obviously like-wise seized. 'Hey, Albert, I believe it.'

'What, my son?'

'That it's haunted. Hey, I don't fancy this at all.' He ducked his head and peered up. 'D'you see where the attic is!'

'Don't tell me it's in the roof! What strange creatures those Victorians were, putting attics in the roof.'

I drew up to the porched front door and cut the engine, the full fury of the rain even more evident in the ensuing silence. Now a jagged multi-fork of lightning ripped the sky and seconds later the earth trembled with a cataclysmic clap of thunder.

'By gum . . .' I said, pounding my chest, 'that was better out than in.'

'I don't like thunder and lightning,' complained Norman,

grimacing at the sky. 'Me granny always turned the mirrors to the wall when it lightninged.'

'Whatever for?'

He shrugged. 'I don't know.'

'If she looked anything like you, I can understand it – but why did she do it only when it lightninged?'

'Cheeky sod,' he grinned.

'Well – are you ready for the dash?'

He shook his head. 'No.'

'Right – on three . . . one . . . two . . . three . . . GO!'

Out we leapt, heads down and knees up, our shoulders soaked immediately. As we ran into the porch another gigantic clap of thunder crippled the sky and Norman stuck his hands over his ears.

I searched for a bell button . . . finally found one under three feet of creeper and gave it a thump. Somewhere in the vast reaches of the house a bell jangled, and while we waited we looked around.

Doom and gloom surrounded us, dense, towering clumps of dark, dripping vegetation and daylight-snuffing trees. It was like a Congo rain-forest.

'How the other half live,' I muttered.

'Which half?' enquired Norman.

'The rich and reclusive, son. These gardens were planted to keep out the eyes of the prying peasants. Personally, I'd rather be gawked at and be able to breathe . . . sssh, someone's coming.'

We heard an inner vestibule door open, then the front door swung inwards.

'Ah . . . Albert, I presume?'

He was about twelve going on forty-six, a slender, studious-looking youth with blond hair and steel-rimmed specs, rather a nice-looking lad, dressed in a plain white shirt and long grey trousers. All very correct and very square. Prep-school from head to toe.

'Otherwise known as Mister Shifty,' I said, putting him in his place. 'And this is Mister Norman, my assistant. You're Geoffrey, I take it.'

'Yes – otherwise known as Master Hyde-Wallace,' he said, putting me in mine.

'We'll make it Geoffrey,' I told him. One thing I can't abide is snotty kids. 'Is your grandfather in?'

'No, he had to go out, but it's all right. Please come in.'

We stepped over the threshold into more doom and gloom, into a tiled vestibule sprouting aspidistras and sporting a wrought-iron umbrella stand not even Fritz would have fancied.

Little Lord Fauntleroy closed the front door and led us into the cavernous hallway, papered in heavy maroon flock, from which a dark, forbidding staircase rose to the first of many floors.

Standing there, I wondered if Hammer used this house for their ghoul films. It was dead right for 'Frankenstein Meets The Werewolf'.

'And what does your grandfather want us to do, exactly?' I asked junior.

'Merely to *tidy* the attic. It's in a frightful state, I'm afraid. I don't think anybody's been up there for fifty years.'

My skin crawled. 'Charming.' I heard Norman gulp. 'And . . . did your grandfather mention anything about payment?'

'No – but he'll be back long before you finish.'

'Not quite the point, young sir – we do not embark upon a job without first coming to an agreement about remuneration.'

'Quite understandable,' he nodded, sounding like the Young Pitt conceding a point on India. 'But if you would like to inspect the job and give me your price, I have been empowered to accept it, up to a certain figure, on his behalf.'

Well, I'll be damned.

'I see,' I said. 'Well, in that case – lead on and we'll take a butcher's at it.'

His studious brow furrowed. 'Butcher's?'

I grinned at him. 'I see they don't include Cockney rhyming slang in your curriculum. Butcher's hook – look. Apples and pears – stairs.'

'Oh,' he said, unimpressed. 'Well, please follow me.'

He started up the stairs, a slender wraith in so large a house.

'Do you live here all alone with your grandfather?' I asked him.

'Yes – when I'm not at school.'

'Bit lonely for you, isn't it?'

'I find plenty to do.'

'Don't you have any pals to play with?'

'One doesn't "play" at my age, one studies.'

'Crikey . . .' Norman muttered behind me.

'Not all the time, though,' I said. 'You must have some fun sometime.'

'I have several hobbies for my leisure moments. I read, collect stamps, listen to records . . .'

'Ah . . . who's your favourite – Gary Glitter . . . David Essex?'

'Chopin,' he said.

I coughed.

'How about sports?' I asked him.

'We have to play them at school, but I'm not frightfully keen. My inclinations are more aesthetic – perhaps even eso-teric – than physical.'

'Fuckin' hell . . .' muttered Norman.

'Yes, I can see that,' I said.

We reached the dark and dismal landing, turned left, and started up a second staircase, the heavens rending with another tumultuous crack of thunder which shook the house.

'Rather a largish house for just the two of you, isn't it?' I suggested.

'We're used to large houses.'

'Hm . . . and your parents?' I ventured.

'On their estate in Scotland. I shall be joining them in the Bahamas later this month.'

'Of course.'

I turned to find Norman with his mouth open.

Up we went to a second landing, along this, then we ap-proached a latched door. Opening it, Geoffrey started up a flight of narrow wooden stairs, the passageway so dark I lost sight of him.

'Couldn't spare a light, could you?' I asked him.

'There's no electricity up here,' he answered. 'But the attic has sky-lights, you'll be able to see quite well.'

'Hey, Albert . . .' Norman muttered quakingly.

'Courage, son.'

'I don't flamin' like this!'

'I'm not all-fired keen meself,' I whispered. 'But I'm damned if I'll let *him* know.'

Up aloft, another door opened and a shaft of dim light filtered down the stairs. 'Here we are . . .' announced Geoffrey.

We stumbled up the last few stairs and gingerly entered the room, my heart sinking at the sight of it.

It was a graveyard of rotting jumble.

'Albert . . .' whispered Norman.

'Yes, Norman?'

'I have just remembered a pressing appointment. I was due at the dentist at eleven o'clock.'

'Well, what do you think?' enquired Geoffrey, giving a three-legged rocking horse a belt behind the ear and starting him in squeaking motion.

'Words fail me,' I told him. 'What exactly are we supposed to *do*?'

'Simply move everything to this end of the room. Grandfather wishes to store some furniture over there.'

'I see. Well, young man, that is no small job. It would certainly take all of today and maybe longer.'

'That is understood. Could you give me a price?'

Well, now – just what sort of limit had the old man in mind? Has the job already been turned down by others? I wondered. It certainly wouldn't have surprised me, it was a real lousy day's work. Come to think of it, I didn't even want it! And I knew Norman was doubly disenchanted.

Right, I thought, I'll really sock it to the kid, state an outrageous price, get turned down – and in ten minutes we could be having a coffee in the Wimpey.

'It's a filthy job, son . . .' I intoned, scratching my chin. 'Don't really fancy it at all.'

He frowned at me, quite shocked. 'But your advertisement did say . . .'

'I know what it said – but naturally we reserve the right to refuse any particular job.'

'Oh, please . . . my grandfather will be most disappointed.'

'Yes, I'm sure . . . well, it's going to be expensive. I don't reckon we could do it under . . .' I glanced at Norman, noted his grimace of disgust, '. . . under a hundred pounds.'

Norman's mouth dropped open, but quickly shut again as he

caught my eye, then he grinned, knowing the price was preposterously high and would be turned down flat. A hundred quid for one day's work!

'All right,' said the kid.

Norman's mouth dropped open again. I stared at the lad. 'Pardon?'

'I said all right. It so happens that was my grandfather's limit, he knew it was an awful job.'

'I . . .' Oh, blimey.

'Well, then,' said Geoffrey, 'I shall leave you to it. We took the liberty of providing cleaning materials – they're in that cupboard – so there's no need for you to go down again. I shall bring you up a cup of tea at half past eleven.'

'Th . . . thank you.'

And then he was gone.

Norman and I stood staring at one another, not knowing whether to laugh, cry or turn somersaults, then, with a shiver, he turned to survey the awful room and, as if on cue, lightning again filled the sky, illuminating the farthest reaches of the ghostly sepulchre.

'Albert . . .' he started to say in a frail, quavery voice, but the remainder was drowned in an horrendous crash of thunder.

I beat him to the door by a split second. 'Oh, no you don't!'

'Al . . . *bert*!' he wailed.

'Get back, you scurvy dog – a deal is a deal!'

'Aw, *Al*bert . . . !'

He slumped, defeated. 'Aw, rotten hell . . .'

'That's better. Besides – think of what you can do with fifty quid.'

He brightened. 'I get half?'

'On this one – yes.'

He took another look at the room and slumped again. 'It still isn't worth it.'

I took another look and slumped with him.

He was absolutely diabolically right.

But at that moment we didn't know the half of it!

CHAPTER FIVE

Well, we started. We got brushes out of the cupboard and swept the extreme left-hand end of the room, a narrow strip that was relatively clear of rubbish, then we started moving stuff into it, sweeping and dusting as we went.

You could not be*lieve* the things old Colonel Whatsit had up there, mostly relics of his military career stretching back half a century or more. There were tables made of elephants' feet, stuffed animals' heads, framed photographs of the British raj, a Watutsi shield and a bundle of spears, cabin trunks, boxes galore, cane furniture, chamber-pots, a wind-up gramophone . . . and so on and so on, eight million tons of ancient bric-a-brac, thick with dust.

'Ah ha!' I exclaimed, snatching up the shield and spear and advancing on a moth-eaten, one-eyed lion's head. 'At last we come face-to-face with the scourge of Bengal, the man-eater of Biteya Nutsoff!'

'Careful, Carruthers,' huffed Norman, donning a topee that came down over his ears. 'Better shoot the blighter from the trees.'

'No, this is between him and me – a matter of regimental honour, Chumley-Gore-Baskerville-Featherstone. He ate my batman last week and the blighter owed me a quid. Take *that*, you swine . . . !'

I gave Leo a jab in the left ear and it fell off in a cloud of dust.

'Sorry, didn't know you'd been poorly. Blimey, everything's rotten up here, Norman . . .'

'Ah ha, Jim, lad . . . rotten as an old ship's biscuit.'

I turned to find him impersonating Long John Silver with an enormous stuffed eagle on his shoulder.

'Well, now, lookee 'ere, Jim . . .' he said, opening the lid of a cabin trunk, 'if it ain't old Bluebeard's treasure chest, chock-ful of . . . ERK!'

He dropped the lid with a crash and shot back eight feet, catapulting the eagle head-first into the wall.

'What's the matter?' I demanded, heart thumping.

'ERK!' he went again, grabbing his throat and tottering around with the horrors. 'It's full of eyeballs! Great, starin' eyeballs! All my slaughtered victims have come back to haunt me . . . !'

'You great narna, you scared the life out of me! Come on, get this stuff shifted and stop fucking about.'

We worked at it seriously for all of ten minutes, but gradually fascination for the old relics got the better of us again.

'Hey, just look at this, Albert . . . !' he said, brandishing a long, curved cavalry sword. 'Bet the old boy was in the charge of the Light Brigade. Cannons to the right of us . . . cannons to the left of us . . . into the Valley of Death rode the six hundred . . . chaaaaaaarrrrrrgggge ! ! !'

With an almighty shout he went thundering down the room, slashing left and right at imaginary foes, then turned sharp left to face a huge old wardrobe standing against the wall.

'Got you, you dastardly swine . . . now fight like a man! Take that . . . and that!'

For a few seconds he slashed wildly at his opponent's blade, then with a triumphant cry drove in an attack, striking the wardrobe door a blow at full stretch.

What happened next was quite comical, because the door began to swing slowly open, on squeaking hinges, and from where I was standing, way down the room, it looked as though his opponent was slowly keeling forward to die.

Norman, keeping up the act, remained frozen in full-stretch position, staring at the wardrobe as though watching his victim demise, then, appalled at what he'd done, he started to come slowly upright, then backed away, his mouth gaping in horror.

'So – you got him . . . now come back and do some work,' I called to him.

But he didn't respond. He stood there frozen, eyes popping, mouth gaping, then . . . crash! he dropped the sabre on the floor. 'Albert . . . !' he wailed.

'Yeah, I know – more eyeballs. Norman, stop screwing about and come back here.'

He began to shake his head slowly. '*Al*bert . . . !' he wailed again . . . and something in his tone sent a shiver through me. This time he wasn't kidding!

The room became very still, horrifically silent, both of us rigid, puzzled, waiting . . . then, with perfect, diabolical timing, a great bolt of lightning seared the scene with blinding, stroboscopic light, illuminating Norman and the wardrobe in a series of flickering, stark-white flashes, then came the thunderclap – a gigantic heaven-splitting detonation. Yet even through this I could hear Norman's wild, tortured cry as he turned, bug-eyed with horror, and came staggering towards me, his arm outstretched, pointing at the wardrobe.

'Al . . . beeeerrtt! It's a *body*!'

My blood froze . . . ice swept through me, my head-hairs tingled and crawled like spiders all over my scalp. 'DAAAAHHHHHH!' I yelled, grabbing his arm. 'Norman, I'll *kill* you . . . !'

'It's true . . . it's *true*!' he cried, shaking, trembling, clutching my arm savagely. 'It's a kid . . . a girl! *Stabbed*! Stabbed through the *heart*!'

We just stood there, rooted, my mind blank with fright, trying desperately to cope with this nightmare, my eyes staring at the wardrobe, my mouth protesting, 'NO . . . ! NO . . . ! NO . . . !'

'IT IS . . . ! IT IS . . . ! GO AND LOOK . . . !'

'NO . . . ! NO . . . !'

Suddenly . . . silence. Dreadful, shocked nothing. Only the rain and our ruptured breathing. I was shaking all through, petrified, still clutching Norman's arm.

'It can't be . . .' I gasped, afraid to speak, afraid to break the silence in case I disturbed the THING. 'Norman, it . . . can't be.'

His voice was a strangled whimper. 'Albert . . . it *is* . . . it's a . . . *corpse*!'

Then he was off, streaking for the door. He yanked it open and disappeared through it, and I was one split-second after him. 'Norman . . . wait!'

Clatter . . . clump . . . thud . . . he was down those stairs eight at a time. Crash! he was through the lower door and along the landing.

'Norman, for CHRISSAAAAAKE! WAIT!'

Deaf and dumb with fear he hit ninety round the bend, four hundred and twenty along the straight, two thousand feet per second down the main staircase – and almost beat me to the front door.

'STOP! THINK! WOA! DESIST!' I cried, prodding him in the chest, my own panic subsiding now in favour of common sense. 'Norman . . .' I gasped, 'just . . . hold on a second . . . this is *crazy*!'

'I SAW IT! IT WAS THERE!' he protested, bug-eyed, terrified. 'ALBERT, IT WAS THERE! . . . There was BLOOD! . . . and the KNIFE was sticking . . .' he gave his chest a thump, over the heart, '. . . in *there*.' He gave a mighty shudder and I thought he was going to faint – or be sick – maybe both.

'Norman, listen . . . *listen* to me . . . it was dark up there . . . you could've been mistaken . . . maybe it was a doll . . . a . . . a pile of rags . . . a Guy Fawkes or something . . .'

He was shaking his head vehemently. 'No . . . no . . . NO! It was a real *kid*! A *girl*! I saw the blood, Albert . . . it was . . . it was WET!'

My stomach lurched. 'Jesus wept . . . Norman, I . . . what the hell are we going to do?'

'Go to the cops . . .' he gasped. 'We've got to get the cops!'

I broke away from him, paced the hall, my mind a maelstrom of bewilderment. It was ridiculous. It was not happening. It couldn't be *real*!

'Norman . . .' I groaned, going back to him. 'Man, it can't *be*!' I pointed up the stairs. 'There cannot be a dead *kid* in that wardrobe!'

'Well, there BLOODY *IS*!' he screamed at me . . . and suddenly I was convinced.

Why couldn't it be? The papers were full of such diabolical things every day. Sinful how you could get used to reading them and never equate them with real-life tragedy and horror. And now we'd stumbled onto something and suddenly it was all very, very different . . .

'The lad,' I said, suddenly rational. 'We've got to find young Geoffrey and get him out of here . . .' I turned and ran along the lower hall, shouting, 'Geoffrey . . . ! *GEOFFREY* . . . !'

Norman, sobered by concern for the boy, joined me, and together we scoured the ground floor rooms, opening door after door, shouting at the tops of our voices.

But no Geoffrey.

'He could've gone out,' Norman suggested.

I frowned. 'In this weather?'

He shrugged. 'Maybe there's a summer house or a garage or something.'

'Come on.' We went quickly through the kitchen, into a scullery, then out through an external door into the rear garden. 'GEOFF . . . REY . . . !' I bellowed.

We ran to the bottom of the large garden, shouting all the way, then scuttled back, soaked to the skin, and sheltered under a rear-door porch.

'He's not here, Norman. He's not in the house. He must've gone shopping or something.'

'Let's phone the cop-shop, Albert,' he pleaded. 'We've got to call the cops.'

'You're right.'

We dived back into the house, shouting Geoffrey's name as we made our way quickly back to the front hall, but there was still no response. In the hall I came to a halt, looked around. 'Where is it?'

'What, Albert?'

'The phone! Try that room there, I'll check this one.'

A minute later we met again in the hall.

Norman shook his head, I shook mine, then, with one mind, we shot down the hall to the rear rooms, the living room, the kitchen . . .

'Where the hell *is* it!' I panted. 'It's got to be somewhere, young Geoffrey called me this morning!'

He gave a gulp. 'Upstairs?'

I ran cold again. 'Forget it. No, Norman, there's got to be one down here, for crissake . . . if there's one at all!'

I was off again, to the front door. I pulled it open, ran out into the rain, gazed skywards, searched this way and that.

'What you lookin' for?' asked Norman, following me out.

'Telephone wires! And there bleedin' ain't any! He must have called from a kiosk!'

'Albert, let's *drive* to the cop-shop! Come on, mate . . .' he pleaded.

I needed no urging. I wrenched open the van door and clambered in, stuck the key in the ignition and started the engine, let out the clutch and started off . . . and almost ran into a flower bed.

The steering was crazy!

'Christ, what's happening?' gaped Norman.

I flung open the door and got out, ran round the front of the van . . . and stared apoplectically.

Both front tyres were flat!

Norman stuck his head out. 'What is it, Albert?'

'Come and look!'

He joined me in the lashing rain, his chin hitting the driveway.

'Eh . . . !'

'Norman . . .' I seethed, 'there's something very, *very* weird going on around here!'

He gaped at me. 'D'you think . . . it *is* haunted?'

'I *think*, old son, I want to get away from here *extremely* fast!'

'But how, Albert?'

'On foot, son! Come on!'

We got lucky with the fourth car that came along – an old crock driven by an even older crock with grey hair and a pince-nez who might have been Margaret Rutherford travelling incognito.

'Where to?' she shouted through her window.

'The nearest police station!' I replied, rain waterfalling down my nose and cascading off my lips.

'Oh, dear!' she exclaimed, her eyes lighting up with interest. 'You're not in trouble, I hope? Come on – get in, get in!'

We clambered in dripping water everywhere.

'Never mind the upholstery,' she said cheerfully. 'It's real leather, it won't come to any harm.'

We squelched down into the rear seat and she started off, the little engine roaring away and getting nowhere.

'*Are* you in trouble?' she persisted, a schoolmarm questioning two pupils.

'No – *we're* not, but somebody is,' I said, reluctant to say too much. 'We've just seen something that needs reporting.'

'Oh? And what's that?'

I glanced at Norman. 'A break-in,' I told her. 'We think we saw a couple of fellas breaking into a house.'

'Oh, how terrible! Well, good for you . . . very public spirited, I'm sure. If more people responded as you're doing, we'd have far less crime in this dear country.'

All the way down Putney Hill she prattled on about crime and hippies and law-and-order, and the further we got from the house, the more unbelievable the situation became.

How could it be happening to *us*!

I glanced at Norman and could see from his bludgeoned expression the same thought was occurring to him. He turned to me and shook his head, then scratched it, no doubt wondering when he would wake up from this nightmare.

'Here you are, boys . . .' she announced, drawing to the curb in the High Street. 'I certainly hope they apprehend those creatures.'

'Thanks very much for the lift.'

We got out and she drove off. Suddenly, standing there, the full seriousness of what we were about to do struck us, mortified us.

'Mate . . .' I said, swallowing hard, 'you're . . . absolutely *certain* you saw . . . ?'

He nodded miserably. 'Pretty sure . . . yes . . .'

'*Pretty* sure!'

'No, no! Abso*lutely* sure, Albert! God's honour!'

'Well, then . . .'

I heaved a sigh, looked up at the police station door . . . and started up the steps.

There were three uniformed cops behind a counter, one standing at it, two at desks. The counter cop glanced up from a ledger as we entered, then came back for a second glance, a grin on his mouth. 'Rainin', lads?' He completed the entry, closed the book, and pocketed his pen. 'Now, then, what can we do for you?'

'I . . .' I began, filled now with dread that we were making an appalling mistake. 'We . . . wish to report a suspected felony,' I said, trying for accuracy – and also to cover ourselves in case of a blow-out.

'Oh?' said the cop, reaching again for his pen. 'What sort of "suspected felony"?'

I glanced at Norman, licked my lips, wiped the rain – or was it sweat – from my brow, swallowed a couple of hard ones and said, 'Murder.'

That got him.

It got the other two, too.

Three sets of brows shot up in surprise, then came down with a clang into frowns of acute interest.

'What's your name, son?' the desk cop asked quietly.

'Alb . . . bert Shifty.'

'And yours?'

'Narna . . . Norny . . . Norman Norman,' stammered Norman.

'Take it easy, no need to be nervous . . . just give me the facts as lucidly as you can.'

'I run a small business,' I told him. 'Our ad's in the local paper – "Odd-jobs around the home – Let Albert Do It".'

The cop nodded. 'Believe I've seen it. Go on . . .'

'This morning I got a phone call . . . from a young lad. He said his grandfather wanted an attic clearing out . . . big house on Victoria Drive . . . house called M . . . Monk's Haunt.'

'Oh, aye . . .' said the cop, scribbling now.

'We went round there at ten o'clock,' I went on. 'The young lad was there . . . name of Geoffrey Hyde-Wallace . . . said his grandfather, Colonel Hyde-Wallace was out, but he'd given the lad the authority to do a deal with us.'

'How old is this boy?' asked the cop.

'I'd say about twelve.'

He frowned. 'Bit young to be negotiating business deals, wouldn't you say?'

I shrugged. 'I suppose so, but he's a very intelligent kid . . . very well educated, you know the type.'

'Go on.'

'Well, he took us up to this creepy attic . . . awful place, full of old rubbish. We didn't like the look of the job, did we Norm? So I decided to ask a lot of money and kill the deal.'

'How much did you ask for?'

'A hundred pounds. I never thought I'd get it.'

'But?'

'The kid agreed – said it was the limit his grandfather had set for the job.'

'Hm mm,' nodded the cop. 'What happened then?'

'The lad left us to it and went downstairs . . . and we started clearing up the mess. Well . . . we got sort of interested in some of the old things up there – military relics that probably belonged to his grandfather – and then Norman found this cavalry sword and started messing about with it . . . you know, pretending he was fighting off the enemy. Then . . . well he started fencing this old wardrobe, a big oak job standing against the wall, and . . . and he touched the door . . . and it opened . . . and inside he saw . . .' I turned to Norman. He was standing in a sort of trance, staring into space, his mouth open, obviously re-living the moment of horror, '. . . tell them what you saw, Norm.'

He gulped, came back to earth. 'It was a kid . . . a girl . . . in a white dress . . . covered all over in . . . b . . . blood . . . with a knife sticking out of her . . . chest.'

That did it.

I mean, that bloody did it!

I've never seen cops move so fast in me life – not even on telly!

I reckon it took no more than thirty seconds before we were hurtling up Putney High Street in the back of a squad car, bells making a hell of a racket, clearing the traffic out of the way like magic, then up Putney Hill at ninety, round the round-a-bout, along Victoria Drive, and into the grounds of Monk's Haunt, long before the full minute was up.

As we skidded to a halt in the gravel driveway, another cop car swirled in behind us and two plain-clothes guys got out, one heading for the front door, the other for the rear of the house.

In our car were three uniformed blokes – the driver and two others, one in the back with us. Now two of them got out, leaving us with the driver.

Through the steamed-up windscreen we watched them assemble at the front door and ring the bell. A few seconds passed and nothing happened. They exchanged conversation. Then one of them spoke into a walkie-talkie and a few seconds later the front door was opened by the plain-clothes detective who'd gone round the back.

They all trooped inside and the front door was closed . . . and then we waited.

'Mind if we smoke?' I asked the driver.

'Sure – go ahead.'

My hands were shaking so badly I almost burned my nose. Norman was even worse.

'I can't believe it's happening, Albert,' he croaked. 'Blimey, only two hours ago we . . .'

I glanced at my watch. Good God, it was only half past eleven! Only an hour and a half since we'd got here. It seemed like days.

'Two hours ago we were having breakfast, mate – and don't I wish we still were! Even Frau Kranki's breakfast!'

Minutes passed. The driver didn't say a word. It was hell.

'Will we get our pictures in the papers?' asked Norman, dead miserable.

I shrugged. 'Maybe.'

The driver spoke for the first time. 'Would you like your pictures in the papers, lads?'

'No, we wouldn't,' I said, smelling a loaded question.

He didn't reply.

Suddenly the front door opened and one of the plain-clothes dicks came up to the car and opened our door. 'All right, lads – inside.'

We entered the hall where the other plain-clothes bloke was waiting for us. 'In here,' he said, pointing to a drawing room. I'd been in it before, looking for the phone.

'Sit down,' he said, and we all sat round a table by the window. 'All right, lads, I just want to go over your story again . . . and this time Mister Norman can tell it. Fire away, Mister Norman.'

Norman repeated it, somewhat nervously, which was understandable, and all the time he was talking I had the feeling the cop didn't believe a blind word he was saying. Mind you, cops are inclined to look like that even when talking to their mothers.

All the way through Norman's recital the cop just kept nodding and muttering 'Hm hm,' and 'Huh huh,' with his eyes narrowed like laser beams on Norman's, as though trying to spook him.

'So . . .' he said, when Norman had finished, 'a harrowing

experience for you, son . . . and one you wouldn't care to repeat.'

'Not likely.'

'Well, I'm sorry, lad, but you're going to have to come upstairs with me and take one more look at that wardrobe.'

I felt sick. Norman paled noticeably. 'Oh, Christ . . .' he muttered.

The cop got to his feet. 'Come on.'

All the way up those three thousand stairs my stomach revolted, and I thought any second Norman was going to turn and run, despite the cop behind us.

We reached the upper landing and started up the last narrow flight of stairs, the prospect of entering that despicable attic again overwhelming me with horror.

There were three cops up there – two in uniform and the other plain-clothes chap who'd met us in the doorway.

'Right,' he said, 'just show us again how you discovered the body.'

I walked off left. 'I was standing over here . . . and Norman picked up the sword . . .'

'Pick up the sword, Norman,' said the cop, 'and do what you did before.'

'Well, I . . . I sort of went down the room like this . . . swishing the sword . . . then I turned to the wardrobe and . . .'

'The door was closed?' asked the cop.

'Oh, yes, shut tight.'

'Go on.'

'Well, I . . . sort of attacked it, pretending it was one of the enemy . . . we were just fooling around.'

'I understand. Okay . . . go on, attack it again – just as you did before.'

Shaking like a jelly, Norman went into a stretching posture and reluctantly pinked the door.

Nothing happened.

He pinked it again, harder this time.

Still nothing happened.

'Oh . . .' he gulped. 'It swung open before.'

'Hm . . .' said the cop. 'Son, *we've* been hitting it for ten minutes and couldn't get it to open once.'

'Well . . . perhaps it wasn't quite shut before?' Norman suggested.

The cop shook his head. 'We've tried that. The floor is uneven, the door won't stay closed-to, it swings open. It's got to be either firmly shut or fully open.'

'Oh . . .' croaked Norman, gawping at me. 'Well, I don't know what happened, then.'

'Mister Norman . . .' said the cop, in a sinisterly quiet voice, 'we have not removed anything . . . and I do mean *anything* . . . from this room since we arrived. As far as we are concerned it is *precisely* as you left it.' He took a step toward the wardrobe, reached for the door catch . . . and opened the door wide.

From where I was standing Norman reacted exactly as he'd done before . . . he gave a start, then froze, mouth open, eyes bulging.

Poor bastard, I thought, why are they making him go through that hell again.

Now he transferred his pop-eyed gape to the cop and stammered, 'B . . . but . . . it's empty!'

My brain exploded.

The cop nodded. 'And not a sign of blood anywhere.'

Norman stared at me, me at him. I strode forward, looked inside the wardrobe. It most certainly was empty.

'So . . .' sighed the cop. 'Perhaps you lads would now care to tell us what this . . . . *game* . . . is all about.'

Norman was mouthing but nothing was coming out.

'Let's go downstairs,' said the cop, a mean edge now harshing up his voice. 'There's one other little mystery we'd like to clear up.'

In a daze we clumped down the stairs to the ground floor, then out through the front door, towards our van.

'You said,' said the cop, 'that you came out and found both front tyres flat, is that correct?'

'Absolutely!' I put in. 'Both down to the rims! That's why we had to thumb a lift . . . to . . .'

I came to a stunned halt, staring at the front tyres.

They were both fully inflated!

'Oh . . . no!' I gasped, now knowing it was all a nightmare – either that or I'd gone off my rocker. Norman was shaking his head from side to side, having obviously reached the same conclusion about himself.

'Furthermore . . .' the cop was saying, in the tone of deadly matter-of-factness they use when they've just collared a prime villain, '. . . we've done some checking on the owner of the house and two interesting facts have come to light. One – that Colonel Hyde-Wallace never *had* a grandson named Geoffrey . . . in fact he never had a grandson named anything. And two . . .' his eyes speared us in turn, making sure he had our undivided attention, '. . . Colonel Hyde-Wallace has been dead for six months.'

Baff!

An icy shiver ripped through my body.

Well, that was it – somewhere during the course of the morning I'd lost my mind . . . maybe up there in that attic. I'd flipped! Lost my slates! This wasn't happening at all – it was all a figment of my crazed mind!

'So – what d'you think of *that* little lot?' enquired the cop.

Silence.

'Hm . . . well, lads, perhaps something will come to you later on. I don't know what you're little game is, but . . .'

'DAAAAHHHHH!' Norman suddenly cried out – and then he was away, running hell-for-leather across the garden towards the gate.

'Oh, no . . .' I groaned. The poor sod had really flipped.

'Stop!' yelled the cop. 'You can't get away, lad!'

But Norman had other ideas. Before any of the other cops could move a foot, he was out through the gate and lost to view.

'Catch him!' bawled the plain-clothes bloke to the others, then turned to the driver. 'Hold this one!'

'I'm not going anywhere!' I protested.

'You're damn right, you're not!'

The driver leapt out and clamped an iron claw on my arm. 'Easy, lad, don't do anything stupid.'

'I'm not going to run! I want this mess cleared up!'

Now the uniformed cops were galloping through the gate after Norman. Poor fool, he didn't have a chance! They'd be on him before he could say handcuffs. What a stupid thing to do, he really must have flipped. Well, no wonder after what he'd been through.

'Bit of a nutter, is he?' enquired the driver.

'No, he's not! He's a good lad, never done anything wrong in his life.'

'Well, he's done it now. What was it – a publicity stunt? Drummin' up a bit of business by getting your pictures in the papers, were you?'

'That's crazy . . . !'

He shrugged. 'Been done before.'

'Well, not by us!'

'Come on, you'd better sit in the car.'

We started towards the patrol car, but as we reached it a troupe of figures marched back through the gate – three cops, Norman . . . and a young boy and girl!

My chin hit the gravel. The young lad was Geoffrey Bloody Hyde-Wallace!

' 'Ello, 'ello, 'ello . . .' muttered the driver, 'what do we 'ave 'ere?' And he steered me towards the on-coming group.

Then, just as we reached them, a little Morris 1000 swirled into the drive-way, pulled up behind the rear squad-car, and an elderly – and very mystified – man climbed out. 'What's . . . what's goin' on 'ere?' he demanded.

The plain-clothes cop who had interrogated us in the attic walked towards him. 'Who are you, sir?'

'I'm . . . Alfred Maddox . . . I live 'ere. What the 'ell's goin' on? What you 'olding my kids for?'

The cop turned to the boy and girl who were now looking extremely crestfallen.

'They your kids?' asked the cop.

'Grandson and granddaughter,' nodded the old bloke. 'What they been up to?'

The cop didn't answer but walked across to the group. 'This the boy?' he asked me.

'That's him,' I sighed with relief.

He turned to Norman. 'This the girl?'

Norman nodded. 'I saw them peering over the wall from next door's garden.'

'Should have let us do the chasing, son, we've had more practice.' He turned to the kids. 'Right little pair of monkeys, aren't you . . .'

86

The old man came forward, belligerently. 'Look, what's this all about, officer?'

The cop told him. As the story unfolded, the old bloke got madder and madder, then finally stepped forward and fetched young Geoffrey a belt round the ear, 'You stupid little bugger!' he bellowed, then went after the girl, catching her a beaut.

Now both of them were bawling their eyes out.

'Can't leave you alone for five minutes!' ranted grandad, turning to the cop. 'It's that perishing actin' school their mother sends them to! They're always making up things and frightening the life out of people! Last week they dressed up as ghosts and scared the bleedin' milkman so hard 'e dropped a crate-load of bottles! Right – get inside, you two, I'm goin' to scare the daylights out of you for a change – with my belt!'

In floods of tears the kids scarpered round the back of the house. As they disappeared, the old man turned to Norman and me, very embarrassed.

'What can I say, lads . . . 'xcept I'm very sorry. I'm only the caretaker here . . . I'm lookin' after the place for Mrs. Hyde-Wallace while she's in hospital . . . poor soul was hit very hard by the colonel's death. The kids . . . ? It's not really their fault . . . the mother's in the theatre, bit of a hippy, she hardly ever sees them. Could be their way of getting attention. Their father did a bunk when they were tots. Very sorry, lads . . . sorry about the money, too. I've got no hundred pounds to give you.'

'Forget it,' I told him. 'We're just very relieved there was no dead child.'

'Little bastards . . .' he seethed. 'What a stupid trick to pull.'

'There better hadn't be any more of them,' the cop warned him. 'Serious business, pulling the police out on a wild-goose chase.' He nodded at me. 'All right, lads, on your way . . .'

Suddenly everybody had gone.

Norman and I climbed into the van, still stunned, and for a moment just sat in silence, staring at the now gently-falling drizzle, everything quiet as the . . . grave.

'Did it happen, Albert?' Norman asked wonderingly. 'Or have we just arrived?'

'Well, if we *have*,' I declared, starting the engine, 'Master Hyde-Wallace can stuff his attic – we're off!'

*   *   *

Cold, wet, miserable, and a hundred quid poorer, we climbed out of the van and entered the portals of Chez Kranki.

'I knew the moment I woke up I should've stayed in bed,' I told Norman. 'I just *knew* this was going to be a real lousy day. Well, that's it for me – I'm going back to bed. No good can possibly come from a day that starts so badly.'

'Oh, Albert . . . !' called the sweet voice of Dillys.

I stopped on the stairs and hung over the bannisters. 'Yes, beloved, what is it?'

She came to the bottom of the stairs and winked up at me. 'There was a call for you while you were out.'

'Not an attic-clearing job, by any chance?'

'No . . . a lady. She wants you to go round on Monday afternoon and give her a quote on a loft-ladder. She lives on the Belview Estate . . .'

My heart stumbled.

'Oh? And what was her name, angel of light?'

'Mrs. Angela Lambert.'

There – who *said* no good could come from a day that started so badly?

'Thank *you*, honey bun,' I grinned. 'I shall be there.'

And, whistling a chorus of 'Oh, What A Beautiful Morning' I continued up the stairs to put my batteries on super-charge.

CHAPTER SIX

Sunday morning at Buchenwald is a carnival of do-as-you-please. The week's hard labour (except in the case of Dan Philby) behind us, we bask in the righteous good-humour of the self-satisfied, taking our reward in licence to dress as weirdly as takes our fancy and take our leisure in no-matter-what momentary whim.

I awoke in sparkling spirits of my own accord (Norman being excused alarm clock duty on Sundays), my well-being not the slightest bit due to the prospect of my visit to the Languid Lambert on the morrow, an excitement which had stayed with me during the hours of slumber and which had resulted in a dream of the most licentious and satisfying nature.

By the heck, I thought as I leapt out of bed, if the real thing even approximates to that dream I shall be hospitalised for a month with a glucose drip stuck in me arm.

Swiiiish! Back went the curtains on a fantastically beautiful day, the sun a blob of molten butter in a sky as blue as a budgie's bum. Could yesterday have happened? It was impossible.

Diving into the drawer for my trusty binocs, I swung them onto a big black crow eating a banana in the garden of 76. Well now, you live and learn . . . I never knew crows ate bananas.

Up now to the chimney of 78, to a thrush having a cough preparatory to bursting into song. There she went, warbling and chirruping away like she'd just come up on Littlewoods, happy soul.

Hello, Dirty Dicky was in the gutter again, chucking muck in the air and letting it fall on his head. What *did* he get out of it? Well, a filthy head, for starters. You wait till you get home, Richard, your ma will whale the daylights out of you . . . aye aye, two blackbirds were having it away on the roof of the bike shed! Sinful, that, on a Sunday. No sense of decorum some birds . . .

Ziiiipp! I whip-panned to Esme's window as her curtains

flew back. Oh, how radiant she looked this morning in an off-the-shoulder creation in daffodil yellow with big pink rosebuds embroidered on the . . . no, they weren't rosebuds, they were nipples!

Three steps back and off it came. By George, she hadn't half got a pair. Esme, love, if only you *knew* what you do to this poor wretch every morning of his celibate life . . . blimey, there she went, straight into the Stork position, a miracle of balance considering the ballast she was carrying in front. Now she struck the Cobra pose, now the Squat, now the Camel (humps on the wrong side), now the Lion . . . the Swan . . .

That's one thing I love about Sundays – she has time to go right through the book.

Yes, and here it came, my all-time favourite – the Angular Balance Pose, where she sits down, grabs her ankles, and shoots her legs out wide, balancing on her coccyx. And if I don't stop this I'll be balancing on mine!

With a farewell groan of frustration, I stowed away the bins, attired myself for the bathroom, and opened the door, finding Norman there in striking pose, about to bash me on the hooter.

'Well, go on if you must,' I sighed.

'Ooh, heck, I nearly did,' he grinned. 'Hey, Albert, I was wonderin' – are you planning to do anything today?'

'Only Esme Pickersgill.'

'Who?'

'Why, what've you got in mind?'

'Well, I was wonderin' if you'd like to go over to Sandown Park for an hour or two.'

I frowned. 'Sandown? One thing I can't stand, Norman, is horse racing. Besides, it's Sunday, they don't race on . . .'

'No, not racing! To the golf driving range. There's a range in the middle of the course. I've heard it's smashing.'

'Golf!' I laughed. 'Are you mad – me play golf! Me – walk ten blinking miles round a . . .'

'No! You don't *walk* anywhere, Albert, you hire a bucket of balls and just stand there, smashin' 'em down the range.'

'What a very odd way to spend Sunday.'

'No, it's luvly, Albert . . . it's a bit of exercise.'

I clutched my bosom. 'Dammit, man, don't mention that

filthy word. One thing I cannot abide is exercise. Horse racing and exercise – two things I simply cannot abide . . .'

'There'll be lots of birds there, Albert.'

'Hm?'

'Birds. There's always hundreds of 'em there . . . swinging away in their tight blue jeans and little short shorts . . .'

'Norman . . .'

'Hee, you should see them wiggle their bums when they're settling in for the swing . . . ching . . . ching . . . ching . . . all wriggly and . . .'

'Eleven o'clock,' I nodded, pushing past him. 'And don't flaming-well keep me waiting.'

*   *   *

'I'm going to play golf,' I told Bennie and he spluttered his cornflakes into his lap.

He looked radiant this Sunday morning in a Hawaiian shirt that resembled a paint factory that had taken a direct hit.

'Golf! You! You haven't got the temperament for it, man.'

'The way *I* play it I have.'

'What way's that – flat on your back in a bunker?'

'Not on *my* back,' I grinned, drawing a tut from Von Brik and a glower from Philby. 'Why don't you come along, Bennie, I bet you're a genius at ball games. You fellows have the rhythm, you know.'

'Baby, I've had more birdies on the golf course than you could shake a nine-iron at. And as for holes in one . . . !'

Crash! went Von Brik's fork. He didn't say anything, just crashed his fork.

'So – come along and show me how it's done,' I urged.

He thought about it, then shook his head. 'Nah . . .'

'There'll be lots of birds there.'

'Hm . . . ?'

'Birds. There's always thousands of them there,' I said, throwing a wink at Norman. 'Swinging away in their tight blue jeans and little short shorts. Boy, you should see them wiggle their . . . see them wiggle when they settle down to swing . . .'

Crash! went Dan Philby's knife. 'Really, this is inexcusable!'

'Oh, dear, you had the fish pie again, Philby?' I sighed. 'You ought to try the devilled kidneys, they're really quite diabolical.'

'Gutter snipe!' he exclaimed, hurling back his chair and exiting in a fury.

I frowned at Bennie. 'Gutter snipe? I didn't know that was on the menu.'

'I concur absolutely!' barked Von Brik, leaping to his feet.

'Oh, you didn't know it either?' I said. 'I wonder what it tastes like?'

'You go too far, young sir!' he snorted, banging down his chair. 'In Jarmany you vould . . .'

'Be put against ze wall und shot – yeah, I know. Good job we won the war, isn't it?'

He strode from the room, puce-cheeked with fume.

'You were saying?' enquired Bennie, earnestly interested.

I stuck a thumb at Norman. 'Ask him – he's the expert.'

'S'right,' nodded Norman, shovelling in half a fried egg and a wedge of black pudding. 'Thousands of 'em. Well, it's the glamour of the scene that attracts them, isn't it? Birds go for golf in a big way.'

'And you absolutely *guarantee* a major turn-out today? insisted Bennie.

Nodding, Norman shoved in the other half. 'We'll be outnumbered nine-to-one.'

'Then what are we sitting here for?'

'I wonder that every morning,' I said, lowering the boom on my rissoles and beans.

*   *   *

The driving range occupies a lovely setting, smack in the middle of the race-course, which, on such a morning, revealed itself to us as a sparkling, emerald-green oasis of dew-fresh quietitude, nought disturbing its peace and tranquillity but the drowsy buzz of busy bees and the inviting distant thock of club against ball.

We abandoned the van in the car-park, crossed the running-track by way of a mobile foot-bridge, and entered the ranch-style club-house, and were at once captivated by the glamour of the game exemplified by the display of first-class equipment and the high-pro advertisements in the reception area.

Here drove Jacklin, there chipped Player, over there putted

the dashing Miller, exhorting the plebs to buy these shoes, that sweater, those clubs, while incidentally conveying the impression that this was all you needed in order to massacre the opposition in the British Open.

'Swell threads,' observed Bennie, fingering a ninety-guinea sweater. 'The price is a bit swollen, too. Where do we make with the balls, Norman?'

'Over here, fellas.'

We approached a counter at which an extremely haveable chicken in a mini-mini was dishing out clubs and baskets of balls.

'Three, please,' ordered Norman. 'Large.'

She backed off a yard or two and went into a crouch for the baskets, upsetting Bennie no end with an eyeful of knickers.

'Steady, man,' I commanded, grabbing his arm.

'Glug,' he gulped, eyes as big as hens' eggs.

'Left or right-handed?' she enquired from the floor.

'Balls?' I frowned.

'Clubs,' she sighed.

I conferred with Bennie. 'Do you hold it left or right-handed?'

'Both,' he grinned, lighting up the room with his teeth.

And simultaneously with some to spare, I reflected – from what Norman had told me.

'Are you sure you *need* a club?' I asked him and he roared with laughter.

We collected the equipment and went out through a door into a long covered-way of stalls, each with its rubber mat and automatic tee-loading device.

The tees nearest the reception were all occupied, so we started down the passage-way, Bennie giving me a nudge as we encountered the first girls, a duo of shapely lovelies in skin-tight jeans and bursting blouses.

'Hee hee!' he chuckled, breaking into a little dance and shaking six balls out of his basket.

'I told you ... I told you!' insisted Norman.

We trekked on, our hopes soaring as we reached the end and found the last two occupied stalls taken by a pair of crackers so divine they made the first pair look like a couple of dray-horses – a red-head and a blonde, both in shorts cut so brief

93

that even standing upright their dear little buttocks were visible.

'Bags this one!' exclaimed Bennie, breaking into a gallop and occupying the stall adjoining the red-head's.

I beat Norman into the next one by a hairsbreadth and, grumbling, he took the third.

'Now, men . . .' announced Bennie in a voice loud enough to attract the girls' attention. 'I am gonna show you how it's done. Placing the ball upon the tee, you stand back a touch . . . about heyah . . . swing the club up heyah . . . an' gracefully stroke the said spheroid two hun'erd yards down the course like this . . . heyah!'

Whooossshh!

He took an almighty flier at it, missed the ball by a good three inches, let go of the club which went sailing away down the range, turned round three times and sat on his arse in the ball dispenser.

The red-head and the blonde collapsed with laughter. Norman and I applauded – and the game was on.

Within three minutes we knew their names – the red-head was Sheila, the blonde Avril – and within five minutes we had them demonstrating how to hit the ball – a spectacular experience from where we were standing, since every time they took up the strike position their shorts shot another three inches up their bums.

Not satisfied with this, however, Bennie sneakily adopted the helpless-male role and soon had the blonde in his stall, standing hard behind him, correcting his grip and swing. Then, moving fast along the seduction track, the crafty sod reversed their positions and now stood hard behind her, and ten minutes after that they decided to go and buy drinks for us all and were never seen again!

Miffed that her mate had done a bunk – or that she hadn't got to Bennie first – Sheila swept off in high dudgeon – ostensibly to go to the loo – and was also never seen again.

And ten minutes after that it started raining!

'Bloody Sundays,' muttered Norman as we drove home. 'Always the rotten same.'

'Never mind, son, there's always one good thing about Sundays . . .'

'What's that?' he mumbled.

'They're always followed by Mondays.'

'Well, there's nothin' rotten special about them, either.'

'There is about this one,' I grinned.

By golly, there was, too.

CHAPTER SEVEN

Monday morning was an agony of waiting, unrelieved even by the distraction of Esme Pickersgill's sensual contortions, because, dammit, she didn't show. Whether her alarm clock hadn't gone off or she'd caught a cold performing in the nod, I don't know, but I had my binocs trained on her window for half an hour and all I got was sore eyelids.

Breakfast, too, was devoid of time-consuming pre-occupation, Von Brik and Dan Philby, finally capitulating to peurility, imbecility and repulsion, taking their meals in their rooms, and Bennie, whose interrogation re his Sunday seduction I had looked forward to with lip-smacking relish, not turning up at all!

And to compound the felony, Frau Kranki's boiled eggs, by some grave error of judgement, were cooked to perfection, affording not even the distraction of a few piquant insults.

All very draggy.

Sending Norman off to wash the van, I retired to my room to while away the morning hours in rest and contemplation, but after three minutes of that I got fed up and decided to walk down to the local shops for a copy of *Playboy*.

Curses again, they were sold out. So I settled for *Titbits* and a bar of Bournville Plain.

What, I considered, constituted 'afternoon'? – which was when Angela Lambert had said she wanted me to call. Technically it was any time after twelve noon, but I felt she didn't mean that early.

I'd make it three o'clock, smack in the middle, thereby seeming neither too anxious nor too desultory. Oh, these things need thinking about.

Between two o'clock and a quarter to three time crawled by so slowly I thought my watch had stopped; then, finally, it was time. With a surge of inner excitement I opened my door and began to descend the stairs, meeting Bennie – or what *used* to be Bennie –staggering up them like a drunk.

'Hey! what happened to you?'

With enormous effort he raised his head and beamed a grin of lascivious triumph, then tripped and fell on his face. 'Oh, man . . . don't make me talk . . . even my teeth are exhausted.'

'You dirty devil,' I grinned. 'Hey, Bennie, aren't you working today? Bennie . . . ?'

He was asleep.

I stepped over him and continued down, encountering Dillys in the lower hall. 'You off, then?' she enquired. 'Fritz . . . NO!'

Fritz skidded to a frustrated halt, threw a longing eye at my ankle, then a filthy one at Dillys, and scuttled back into the kitchen.

'He'll have problems when he grows up,' I told her.

'Won't we all,' she sighed. 'Will you be in for dinner, Albert?'

'No, love, I'm going to the pictures.'

'Huh!'

'See you,' I grinned.

I piled into the van and found a note from Norman stuck on the steering wheel. 'If you're not home in a week – send wages.'

A week. Now there was a thought.

Fifteen minutes later I was turning into the Belview Estate, wondering what my reception was going to be like. She'd play it cool, I decided, she was the type. Everything nice and easy to start with, all very business-like, then, when I'd inspected the loft, we'd have a cup of tea and chat about this and that, our mouths saying one thing but our minds full of the other. Perhaps nothing would happen at all this first visit. Well, that was fine with me . . . slowly, slowly, catchee pussee.

I drew up at the house, locked the van (just in *case* I didn't see it again for a week), then walked up the driveway and rang the bell.

As soon as the door opened I knew all my premonitions of 'cool' were way off target. She looked hotter than chilli con-carni and twice as saucy in shrink-wrapped black trousers and a white silk blouse, beneath which it was blindingly obvious she wore nothing but breasts.

'Hi,' she smiled, her voice a furry purr, her lazy grey eyes an open invitation to indescribable hanky-panky. 'Come on in.'

As I crossed the threshold she said, 'I thought you weren't coming. I've been waiting ages.'

'Oh? Oh, I'm sorry . . . you didn't say any particular time.'

She closed the door and leaned against it, blow-torching me with the eyes. 'I didn't know if you'd have another job. I imagined you'd get here as early as you could.' She pretended a pout. 'I'm rather hurt.'

I grinned flutteringly. 'No need to be. It's been the longest day of my life . . . waiting.'

She arched a brow. 'Well, now, that's better.' She pushed away from the door and came towards me, all hips and hot seduction, boiling my innerds. I was trembling all over. There was no messing about with this lady, she came straight in, no time-waiting prevarication, an old hand at the game. Her arms snaked around my neck and for a moment she just hung there, grinning up at me, giving the heat of her body time to ooze through my trousers and warm the heart of my cockles, then she came the rest of the way and placed a red-hot poultice of lips on my mouth, completely completing my undoing.

Boing! Up went the starting tapes for a two-horse race, stallion versus brood-mare, a race that I knew would be a marathon of endurance and duration, for this was no ordinary mortal woman. This was a love goddess! A celestial raver!

'Nice,' she whispered approvingly, her hand floating down to encompass old Rod who, knowing it was happy time, had leapt to attention, ready for the thrash of a life-time. 'Wow . . .' she chuckled excitedly. 'Look who just woke up.'

Giving him a squeeze, she sucked air in between clenched teeth then giggled, 'This is wonderful . . . I don't know where to start first.'

'We've got plenty of time for everything.'

Her eyes flared. 'Have we? How much time *do* we have?'

'It's up to you. I'm as free as a bird.'

'Then there's no problem.' She eased away and caught my hand. 'Come . . . let's have a drink.'

She led me into the kitchen and pointed to a stool at a peninsular bar. 'Sit down. What would you like to drink?'

'What are you having?'

'Vodka tonic over ice.'

'Terrific.'

Still trembling, though settling down a bit now, I lit a cigarette and watched her prepare the drinks. She was very watchable – neat, deft, feline, a cat in action, immensely sexy.

She came over with the drinks and hit me with a quick, fiery kiss as she sat down. 'That's just to keep the pot boiling.'

'I like the fuel you use.'

She laughed, raised her glass. 'I like you.'

'I like you, too.'

'Do you?' She took a cigarette and held it to my flame. 'What do you like about me?'

'Everything . . . and not least your directness.'

She nodded, almost aggressively. 'I made up my mind a long time ago that if I wanted something badly enough I'd go out and get it. I wanted you badly, so . . .' she grinned, '. . . well, you're here.'

'Why me?'

'Why not you? You're a nice-looking man. Besides – you come highly recommended.'

'Oh? From whom?'

'As if you didn't know.'

I laughed. 'And how is Mrs. Pinkerton?'

'Right now – ecstatic I should think. She left for Majorca yesterday. You must think we're a couple of kooks.'

'Not at all. I think you're both terrific. I'm awfully glad I put that ad. in the paper.'

She grinned wickedly. 'You may live to regret it . . . when I'm finished with you.'

The rumpus started up again inside and my right leg started juddering. 'And . . . what do you have in mind?'

She gave a playful shrug. 'Who knows? I'm going to play it by ear . . . now that it's started off right.'

'Oh? You feel that, hm?'

She nodded. 'It's perfect. It might not have been, you know. What was good for Vickie might not necessarily be right for me.'

'True.'

'And the same goes for you, of course.'

'True again. Fortunately, it would appear that such fears were groundless.'

'Yes . . . completely,' she smiled, and drank her drink. 'Are you . . . excited, Albert?'

I laughed. 'I'm a nervous wreck!'

'What was your reaction when you got the message that I'd called?'

'I . . . I was delighted. You've no idea how long the week-end has been.'

'I'm very glad. But tell me what you really *thought*.' She hit me with a teasing grin. 'Don't tell me you didn't give your sexual fantasies free rein . . . didn't paint lurid pictures of what would happen?'

'No . . .' I grinned. 'I won't tell you that. Is that what you did?'

'Never mind me, we're discussing you. I'll tell you mine later . . . maybe. Go on – tell me.'

'Oh, I . . . I visualised you as you were the last time I saw you – sunbathing in Vickie's garden in your bikini . . . lying upside down.'

She frowned. 'Upside down?'

'I was looking down on you from Vickie's bedroom.'

'Oh, you were, were you?' she smiled. 'We wondered whether you'd be able to resist the temptation.'

'I couldn't.'

'We knew it.'

'How?'

'Because you look what you are – and have subsequently proven yourself to be, Albert Shifty – a *very* horny gentleman.'

'Oh,' I grinned. 'I wasn't aware it was that obvious.'

'Huh! It's obvious – particularly to those on the look-out for such things. But go on – you were thinking about me in my bikini.'

'Sure.'

'And?'

'Well, I . . . visualised you wearing it when you answered the door, and . . . well, you weren't wearing it for too long afterwards.'

'I removed it.'

'No. I removed it.'

'Sounds fun. And . . . ?'

'I . . . took you upstairs . . .'

'And?'

'Laid you on the bed . . .'

'And?'

'I . . . I'd much rather show you.'

'How very forward of you. Have another drink.'

She got up, took the glasses, saying over her shoulder. 'I've thought about you all week-end . . . and not only thought. I've also planned and schemed.'

'Oh?' I gulped, throat thick. 'Planned and schemed what?'

She turned, smiling. 'To achieve the maximum potential from a perfect situation.' She poured the drinks and returned. 'Cheers.'

'Cheers.'

She reached for another cigarette. 'It's a rare opportunity, Albert . . . far too wonderful to spoil with false pretences, false modesty, false inhibitions. Be honest with him, I told myself, right from the start. Hit him with both barrels as he comes through the door, don't waste precious time playing footsy.'

'You certainly did hit me. That was a broadside!'

'So was yours,' she said quietly, her eyelids drooping. Holding my gaze, she came off the stool and around the bar. I stood to meet her. She took my face in her hands and brought her mouth to mine, her tongue a rattler's tail, filling my mouth, plunging down my throat, one hell of a tongue, seeking adventure, new territories to conquer.

Her hand fell to my zip, expertly located the tag, drew it down. In plunged her gentle fingers, swiftly extricating old Throbbers from the restriction of my shorts and bringing him out into the fresh air.

She lowered her eyes to him, studied him, her brow furrowing with gratified amazement. 'Ohh . . .' she whispered softly, then quickly fell to her knees and held him against her cheek. 'Oh, Albert . . .'

With a muted groan she turned her face and ran her fervent lips along his length, then, reaching his bursting head, opened her mouth wide and swallowed him. Now her tongue leapt to life, spun dizzily around the knob, darted hither, thither, tickled, wiggled, wriggled and probed, finally lancing into my errogenous zone and sending me through the slates.

'Yow! Hey, love . . . !'

She chuckled warmly, removed him, kissed him, pressed him to her cheek, murmuring joyously, 'He's wonderful . . . wonderful . . . and all mine!'

'All yours, love.'

'To do with as I wish?'

'Anything your little heart desires.'

'Imagine . . .'

Her fingers flew to the buttons of her blouse . . . snick . . . snick . . . she flung it wide, releasing magnificent breasts, fullsome, lush and stiffly-nippled. Her arms now encircled me, drawing me close, and thrusting the Rod into the warm embrace of those adorable dumplings.

'Does that feel good?' she whispered urgently, folding her breasts round him like two halves of a bun round a hot dog.

'F . . . Fantastic,' I croaked.

Quickly now, with a new thought in mind, she came to her feet, caught my hand and we were off, out of the kitchen, up the stairs and into the bedroom. While she was drawing curtains, I was shedding threads, and in two shakes of a bee's bum she was also in the raw.

Pow! Clamped together like Siamese twins we hit the bed, kissing, sucking, biting, snuffling, eating each other alive and enjoying every mouthful. Then suddenly onto her back she went, one foot on the mantlepiece and the other up the road. 'Darling . . . quickly!'

Tally ho!

Bearing 240 degrees south . . . ready . . . aim . . . FIRE!

In he went like a bayonet through hot butter, up to the hilt in one glorious plunge.

'Oh, GOD!' she cried ecstatically, wide-eyed with wonder. 'Oh, *ALBERT* . . . !'

Wooomf!

Up into me she drove . . . wooomf! . . . and wooomf! again, her motor beginning to fire on all twelve cylinders. Out of the pits she came, tyres screaming, exhausts roaring. By golly, she went berserk, pounded that bed like a pile-driver, bit and hugged and pummelled and tugged, cried and groaned and shrieked and moaned, then suddenly . . .

'Oh, Christ, I'm coming! Albert, I'm . . . DAAAAAAAA-HHHH! OHHHH . . . ! *OHHHH* . . . ! Oh, God, that's fantastic! Keep going . . . KEEP GOING . . . ! Oh, my *God*, Albert . . . I'm . . . DAAAAHHHHHHHHH . . . !'

'Again!'

'Yes . . . yes . . . YES! There's no stopping me now! I'll just keep having them until you . . . ohhh . . . OHHHHH! . . . DAAAAAHHHHHH! Oh, Albert, fuck me, fuck me, *fuck me* . . . ! DAAAAAAHHHHHH . . . ! Oh, God, oh God . . .'

She was unbelievable! Four – in the wink of an . . .

'*DAAAAAAAHHHHHHH . . . !*'

Five! – in the wink of . . .

'*YOOOOOWWWWWW . . . !*'

Six! In the . . .

'*GOD*almighty . . . !'

Seven! In . . .

'AL . . . *BEEERT* . . . !'

'Yes . . . love!'

'Backwards! Then *really* watch me go!'

All change! Face down everything else up in the air. POOOOOWWWW!

'*OH*, my God . . . now you've done it! Go . . . *GO*!'

I was off – but, by heck, she was way out in front.

'OHHH . . . ! AHHH . . . ! Albert, I . . . *YAAAAAA-HHHH!*'

Eight! A beaut – right from the heart.

'Oh . . . love!' I gasped.

'You too?'

'Ban . . . zaaaaiiii!'

'Terrif . . . ! OHHHH . . . !'

'AHHHH . . . !'

'EEEHHH . . . !'

'OOOOOH . . . ! AL . . . *BEEEERT* . . . !'

'I'M WITH YOU, BA . . . BYYYY . . . !'

WWHHHHHOOOOOSSSSHHH!

'Oh . . . *BOY* . . . !' she cried. 'Oh, Albert, that is . . . oh, wow, that is just . . . oh you big . . . randy . . . bull!'

Laughing, I collapsed against her, she subsiding with a comical groan, taking me down with her to lie behind her, holding her tight.

'Albert . . . Shifty,' she panted, 'you ought to be ashamed of yourself . . . going round making a mess of girls like that. *Aren't* you ashamed of yourself?'

'Sincerely ashamed . . .' I gasped. 'And I promise not to do it ever again.'

She reached behind and slapped me on the bottom. 'Then get the heck out of this bed.' With a satisfied mew she wriggled into me. 'Mmmmm . . . you feel good back there.'

'So do you . . . soft as swans down.'

'We fit rather well, don't you think?'

'Like spoons in a drawer.'

She chuckled and hugged my arm. 'That . . . Mister Shifty . . . was one *hell* of a good go.'

'Unbelievable. *You* were unbelievable.'

'Well, you turned me on.'

'No kidding! If I hadn't hit the buffers, I reckon you'd still be having them!'

'Well, I'm one of the lucky ones.'

'So I gathered. You know, I read an article the other day that said fifty percent of women – including married women – have never had an orgasm. I find that hard to believe.'

'It's true. I know a few women on this estate who haven't. Then again . . .' she grinned, '. . . they haven't been to bed with you. Maybe I'll do them a big favour and recommend you.' She turned onto her back and gazed at me. 'No – to hell with them, let them find their own cure.' Smiling, she kissed me on the nose. 'You're a very sexy fella, Shifty.'

'I . . . do admit I rather enjoy it. And you know I have the sneakiest feeling you do, too.'

'Me . . .' she sighed. 'I *adore* it. I was born sexy. I couldn't wait to screw my first man.'

'How old were you?'

She shrugged, comically. 'Eight. No, I was fourteen.'

I laughed. 'Who was he?'

'A farmer's son . . . thirteen years old but big for his age – and I'm not talking about his height. We did it in a barn in the hay. I just *loved* it. That *gorgeous* sensation when he pushed it into me . . . so hard and strong . . . hot and throbbing . . . filling me until I thought I'd burst.' She gritted her teeth and shivered. 'Wow . . .'

Feeling a stirring against her thigh she eased away from me and looked down, grinning with delight. 'That's my boy,' she whispered excitedly. 'I was hoping he'd hear the call.'

Her eyes met mine, telling me what she wanted, and without a moment's hesitation I rolled on top of her and entered her.

'Oh, Albert,' she gasped, clawing my shoulders.

'That the feeling?' I grinned.

'Exactly,' she nodded. 'No . . . don't move . . . just let me enjoy you.'

Remaining braced but still, I watched her working on me for her own pleasure, finding the experience exciting in the extreme. Summoning full concentration, eyes tight closed, brow furrowed, she zeroed in on the iron hard core that lay deep within her and, using the minimum of pelvic movement, quickly produced, through sustained pressure alone, a shockwave of sexual thrill that caused her to cry out with alarm.

Now she jerked massively, reflexively, and with the movement was devoured by the compulsion to work, to thrust, to drive . . . and within three strokes she came, gloriously.

'WOW!' she cried out, and collapsed with an incredulous laugh. 'Oh, *BOY*, was that something!' She stared up at me, wonderingly. 'Hey, what're you *doing* to me?'

'Me?' I grinned. 'Nothing! I'm just an innocent spectator.'

She squeezed Rodney affectionately with powerful muscles. 'It's him, he's the culprit.'

'Shall I take him home?'

'You wouldn't reach the door alive.'

'Okay, we'll stay.'

'Albert . . . ?'

'Yes, love?'

'I do believe I'm going to make a pig of myself this afternoon, do you mind?'

I shook my head, grinning. 'Be my guest.'

'I must warn you I'm in the mood to make quite unreasonable demands upon your person.'

'And I'm in the mood to accept the challenge. So – let's roll back the carpet and see what happens.'

Smiling gleefully, she nodded. 'Consider it rolled. Boy . . . what an afternoon *this* is going to be!'

CHAPTER EIGHT

And what an afternoon it was.

We dillied, dallied, doodled and dozed – then woke up and did it all over again. She was insatiable, and her appetite for it spurred me on like I've never been spurred before. Everything about it was right. We were totally at ease together, completely free of inhibition or embarrassment, two loving lovers alone on a deserted suburban paradise island, secure from all inhibiting conventions in the privacy of our little world.

At one point, rested and refreshed, she got off the bed, padded naked across the room to her dressing table and stood there, a goddess, brushing her hair, as unconcerned as if she'd been fully clothed.

'What are you looking at?' she smiled at me through the mirror, knowing damn well.

'You. Your fabulous body. You're a feast for the eye, Angela. I could happily lie here for ever watching you.'

'You look pretty good yourself, lying there all naked and naughty.'

'I thought naked men weren't supposed to interest women overly much.'

'Who told you that.'

'I read it somewhere.'

She shrugged. 'Some women, maybe. Then again, maybe *they* don't have much to look at. I certainly have.'

I nodded a bow. 'Thank you, ma'm. Come here and say that.'

'No.'

'I dare you.'

'No! I'm brushing my hair.'

'I'll brush it for you.'

'Huh – which hair?'

I laughed. 'That's rude.' I patted the bed. 'Come and sit here, I promise not to touch you.'

'Oh, sure.'

'Scout's honour.'

'You were in the Scouts? That's a laugh. There must have been a great epidemic of pregnant Girl Guides around that time.'

I shook my head. 'No, I was a virgin in those days – until I was twenty-one in fact.'

'Ha!'

'Come and sit here, Angela,' I pleaded, my fingers itching for her.

With a sigh of mock-reluctance, she capitulated, came over and sat on the edge of the bed, continuing to brush her hair.

'That's better,' I said, allowing my right hand to rest platonically on her right thigh.

'Now!' she threatened, brandishing the brush.

'I'm only touching you.'

'I know what you're only. Behave yourself, you need a rest.'

'I've had one. I feel terrific,' I said, sliding my hand a few inches higher.

With apparent unconcern she went on brushing, raising her arms to reach the back of her head and simultaneously offering her breasts in irresistible profile.

My hand rose of its own accord to cup her right breast, to luxuriate in its softness and warmth, my finger and thumb enclosing her nipple which hardened and puckered at my touch.

Still affecting unconcern she continued brushing . . . and I continued caressing, then suddenly threw in a sneaky squeeze which brought her to heel with a gasp.

'Hey . . . !' she whispered. 'Stop that.'

'All right,' I said, and leaned in to replace my hand with my mouth.

'Ohhh . . .' she groaned, running her fingers into my hair and kneading my scalp. 'That's not fair, you know what it does to me . . . and I was going to have a bath.'

'Good . . . I'll have one with you.'

'Would you?'

'Try and keep me out.'

We entered the bathroom. She turned on the taps, and poured green, perfumed bath-oil into the gushing water, then, while the bath was filling, she turned and wilfully pressed her body against mine, bringing up the Rod gigantically. Now, as she kissed me passionately, she opened her legs and mounted me, biting my lip as he slid up into her. 'Oh, Albert . . .' she gasped, grinding vibrantly against me. Suddenly her knees buckled and with a stifled cry she went limp. 'Oh, *God* . . .'

'Did you come?' I gaped, and she nodded against my shoulder. 'My God, that was quick.'

'It's you!' she cried, thumping my shoulder. 'And *him*! You're a pair of devils, you've got me hooked on you!'

'Terrific.'

'Will you kindly get *out* of me!' she complained, disengaging herself. 'Just look at you, it's disgusting walking round like that. I'll have nothing more to do with you.'

She stepped into the bath, shut off the taps and sat down. I sat behind her. 'Give me the soap, I'll do your back.'

'And *only* my back.'

'Of course.'

I filled the sponge and trickled warm, oily water down her spine, causing her to groan with pleasure.

'You're a sinfully sensuous woman, Angela Lambert.'

'I'm not. I'm perfectly average.'

'Oh, sure. And I suppose it's perfectly average for a woman to have twenty-five orgasms in one afternoon.'

'I did not.'

'No, come to think of it, it's nearer thirty.'

'Don't be ridiculous. I've only had . . .' she gave a shrug, '. . . five.'

'Your arithmetic is lousy.'

'Well, it's you . . . doing those awful things.'

I slid my soapy hand beneath her arm and captured her nipple again. 'Like what?'

She slapped at my hand. 'Like dammit that! Now, stop it!'

But I didn't stop. I continued soaping her breast, gently teasing her nipple between finger and thumb and it took but a moment to ignite her fire. With a helpless groan she relaxed back against me, capitulating to my ministrations while spiritlessly protesting, 'No, Albert, no . . .'

'Nice?' I whispered into her ear.

'No, it's awful . . . you mustn't . . . oh, God, you're making me come again . . .' In mounting torment she rolled her head, clutched my knees, then suddenly grabbed my left hand and thrust it between her legs, climaxing almost immediately. 'Oh, no . . . no!' With a tortured groan she collapsed against me. 'This is ridiculous, you're going to kill me!'

'But what a way to go.'

'Albert . . . ?' she cried piteously.

'Yes, love?'

'I *want* you . . .'

'Yes, love.'

'Here . . . ! Now . . . ! Backwards . . . !'

'Yes, love.'

It's that damned oil, you know, it does it every time. Well, think what it does to you on your holidays.

*   *   *

When we woke this time it was dark.

I felt her stir from my side and lean across to the luminous alarm clock.

'What time is it?' I croaked.

'Ten o'clock! We've been asleep for three hours!'

'I'm amazed we woke at all.'

Chuckling, she came back and sprawled across me. 'How're you feeling?'

I kissed her on the nose. 'Starved.'

'Hey, yes – we haven't eaten anything!'

'Has there been *time*? What do you fancy?'

'You.'

'To *eat*.'

'You.'

She pecked me on the chest. 'What do you fancy?'

'Oh . . . something on toast?'

'Boy, you *are* easy to live with.'

She rolled off me, put on a bed-side light, got off the bed and went to a wardrobe, took out a couple of bathrobes and threw one at me. 'Here – hide your pushy friend while we eat or we probably won't.'

She covered her lovely body in a robe of clingy, cream satin, managing to conceal nothing. I got out of bed and put on the yellow towelling job, not caring much for the idea that it belonged to her husband – whoever and wherever *he* was.

Reading my expression, she smiled. 'Don't worry, he doesn't live here any more.'

'Oh,' I said, feeling better. 'Are you divorced, Angela?'

'Separated – at the moment.'

I frowned. 'Oh?'

'Why – what's the matter?'

'Oh, it was just something Vickie Pinkerton said – about your husbands not wanting you to work.'

'That's right, they didn't. Now my lawyer has advised me not to until the divorce comes through – says it might affect the settlement.'

'Oh.'

She slipped her arm into mine and we made for the door. 'Let's not talk about it, I'm having too good a time.'

'Sure.'

'Though if it helps – *he* left *me* . . . for a Birmingham girl who has just produced his child – O.K.?'

'I'm sorry.'

She shrugged. 'C'est la vie.'

We descended to the kitchen.

'Go make a couple of drinks while I bash about in here,' she commanded, steering me towards the lounge.

While I made two vodka tonics I thought about her, about her situation. It sounded as though she'd been denied conjugal goodies for quite a while. No wonder she was ravenous for it. To a woman like her even one celibate week would seem an eternity, so it wasn't surprising she was clawing the paper off the walls.

By heaven, I began to feel quite public-spirited.

I returned to the kitchen.

'Scrambled eggs all right?' she asked, taking her drink.

'My favourite food – except at Frau Kranki's where they constitute a danger to life and limb.'

'And who on earth is Frau Kranki?' she laughed.

'My beloved landlady who I suspect is an ex-Gestapo Ober-leutnantfuhrer and camp cook of Stalagluft Three. Her scrambled eggs could have won Germany the war. If they'd been dropped on Britain instead of five-hundred-pounders, we'd have surrendered the next morning.'

She laughed, spilling her drink. 'Oh, they can't be that bad.'

'They're worse. Oh, I admit they have their uses – for patching a hole in your shoe, wedging doors open, repairing brick walls . . .'

'What sort of place is it —a boarding house?'

'Loosely — yes. A five-storey Victorian job with all the charm of a slaughter-house. I live — if that's the word — on the top floor, next door to my assistant, Norman.'

'Are there many others in the house?'

'Inmates? Yes, plenty. It's like a rabbit-warren.'

She smiled slyly. 'Any girls?'

'Not the kind you mean. There *is* a landlady's daughter . . . nice kid, built like a Russian discus-thrower.'

'Hm. Nothing doing there?'

I shook my head. 'Not my type — I prefer them skinny.'

'Than-*kew*. For that you'll get your eggs cooked a la Kranki. So — you lead a very celibate life, hm?'

'The word is monastic. The pope gets more than I do.'

'A likely story.'

'It's the truth!'

'So how come you're in such good form? You must train somewhere. Do you meet a lot of lonely, frustrated housewives in your job?'

'No.' She pulled a face. 'Honest!'

'Well, you've come to the right place now. There are some *very* twitchy ladies on Belview.'

'So Vickie was telling me. She said she'd invite me to one of the infamous Belview parties some time.'

'Hey — what a great idea!' She gave a sudden start, as though something had just occurred to her. 'Better *still* . . .'

'What now?'

'The Freddie Armstrong party! This Saturday! Hey, terrific . . . !'

'Who's Freddie Armstrong?'

'A legend in his own lifetime — at least that's how he sees himself. He's an East End barrow boy who's made a million out of scrap iron. Three years ago Freddie and his wife Millie actually lived on this estate — number 398. Then, two years ago, he made an overnight fortune through some gigantic fiddle involving six oil-tankers — don't ask me the details — and he bought a *fantastic* house in Kingston, right on the top of Nob Hill. It really is a beautiful place.'

'You've been?'

'Oh, sure, lots of times. Freddie's one of those characters who "never forgets his old mates", so every now and then he throws one heck of a party and invites most of Belview to it.' She laughed. 'Boy, they are terrific parties. You've never seen so much booze and food.'

'Sounds like fun.'

'Would you like to go?'

'I'd love to.'

'All right, I'll ring Millie and ask her. She'll just *love* you.'

'Oh? Why?'

She gave me a bitchy smile. 'You're her type – young and good-looking. She's crazy about young, good-looking men – which, considering Freddie, is not surprising.'

'Why, what's he like?'

'Ee . . . *normous*. I don't see how he could physically *do* it, even if he got the urge, which according to Millie he doesn't.'

'Oh . . . another frustrated lady.'

She laughed. 'Voracious is the word. You'll have to be careful, once she sets eyes on you, you may never be seen again.'

The old heart took a tumble. 'And . . . what's she like?'

'She's cute – a busty little blonde with a bubble cut, younger than Freddie, in her early thirties. She's very nice but she went off the rails a bit when the money arrived. She gets quite depressed wondering how to spend it.'

'Maybe she'd be interested in a loft-ladder,' I grinned. 'I'll have to put it to her.'

Her eyes hooded. 'I've no doubt she'd love you to put it to her – but watch out for Freddie, he's the jealous type – especially towards young, good-looking fellas. They have the two things his money can't buy – youth and looks.'

'I'll remember.'

She spooned the scrambled eggs onto two plates and brought them over to the counter. 'Hope these are *some* improvement on Frau Kranki's.'

I shook my head. 'I'm afraid they're the wrong colour, Angela . . . they should be sort of . . . browny grey, not bright yellow. You just haven't got the Kranki touch, I'm afraid.'

Smiling, she sat opposite me and regarded me over the rim

of her glass. 'You look very much at home sitting there. I must say it's awfully nice to have a man around the house.'

'It's nice being here. I'm having a lovely time.'

'How are the eggs?'

'Fantastic. They melt in my mouth.'

She grinned wickedly. 'I know how they feel.'

'Now, don't get me going again – at least not until I've finished this.'

'Okay . . . until you've finished that.'

'You're naughty,' I said, feeling it all begin to bubble up again between us. By God, what an appetite she had. I was beginning to think that perhaps she *was* insatiable!

'Tell me . . .' she said softly, reading my mind. 'Do I . . . frighten you?'

I stared at her. 'Hm? Good God, no. Why should you?'

She shrugged. 'It has happened. It's just that . . . I need an awful lot of it.'

I grinned. 'Terrific! Why shouldn't you?'

'Well . . . there *are* accepted norms, you know.'

'Normal to whom? A sex-drive is a highly personal thing, isn't it – what's a lot for one is only so-so for another. I read an article recently about a Manchester solicitor who *had* to have it six times a day – *every* day! Okay, that might seem a terrific amount of sex to some men, maybe to most men, but not to the guy who needs it *eight* times a day.'

'Did they give the solicitor's address?' she grinned. 'He sounds like my kind of man.'

Wow. 'You need it that often?' I grinned, continuing the joke.

She demurred with a purse of her lips, telling me it was no joke.

Blimey, what *had* I run into!

'Eat your eggs,' she smiled, merely toying with hers. 'I didn't mean to quench your appetite.'

'You . . . haven't,' I lied. 'I guess I'm not as hungry as I thought. But they're delicious . . .'

'Albert . . .' she sighed, her tone quite woebegone. 'I think you'd better go home.'

'Hm? Why?'

'Because you . . . do things to me, sitting there.'

I gulped. 'What . . . sort of things?'

She got off the stool and came round, caught my face in her hands and kissed me fiercely, then, with a moan, thrust her hand into the fold of my robe.

'Albert, I want you again . . . I want you all the time!'

'That's . . . fine with me,' I croaked, heart thundering.

'Come – quickly!'

She pulled me into the lounge, released my hand, flew around drawing curtains, then feverishly threw off her robe as she returned to me. Swish! Away went mine.

Grabbing my hand she pulled me down onto the lambswool rug and in a wink had straddled and mounted me.

'Oh . . . *Al*bert . . . !' she cried, sucking in air. 'Oh, that's fan*tastic* . . . ! Oh, *love* . . .' And away she went at a frantic canter, teeth clenched, eyes shut tight. 'Ohhhh . . . Ohhhhh . . . Ohhhh . . . *Ohhhhhh* . . . !'

She hit a beauty, went berserk, then suddenly rolled sideways, onto her back, hauled me between her legs, and away we went again.

POW! She was straight into another one, then through it and racing for her third. God, was there no *end* to her capacity!

'Oh, Albert . . . *Albert* . . . !' she wailed, crazed with lust, demented with ecstasy. 'More . . . more . . . *more*! Fill me! Kill me! *RAPE ME* . . . !'

Jeezus, I was doing me best! But there was no satisfying her! She just kept on having them, taking all I could give her and yelling for more!

'*DAAAAHHHHHH* . . . *!*' she bellowed, notching up her fifth. 'Go . . . go . . . GO!'

'Angel . . . aaa! I can't . . . hold . . . on . . . any . . .'

WHOOOOSSSSHHHHHH!

'. . . *oh*, boy . . .'

'Wonderful . . . ! Gorgeous . . . ! Super . . . ! Terrific . . . ! Fan*tastic* . . . !' she laughed wildly.

Crump! My head hit the floor.

I lay there boneless, exhausted unto death, gasping for breath, numb from the neck down. 'Ye Gods . . . I think I just died.'

'I know you just shot *me*,' she chuckled. 'Oh, Albert, I

needed that . . . *needed* it. Trouble is, it was so damn good I'm going to need it again!'

My heart quailed within my bosom. A fear that had already pricked me now began to overwhelm me as a stone-cold certainty – the fear that I'd landed a five-star, rip-roaring, fully-paid-up nympho! I mean a thrash is a thrash but this was turning into a bleedin' circus! – with me as the main attraction!

'Oh . . . ?' I gulped.

She laughed cruelly. 'Oh, don't worry, I shall give you a nice long rest . . . at least fifteen minutes.'

'F . . . fifteen?'

She shrugged. 'Okay – twenty.' She laughed tauntingly. 'Now, don't tell me you're finished for the night, Albert.'

'Well, I . . .' I croaked, '. . . well, no . . .'

Blimey, we'd been at it for eight flaming hours, what did she expect!

'Oh, don't tell me you're going to break up the party *now*,' she pouted, teasingly. 'Still . . .' she sighed, 'I suppose it is getting late and you do have to get home before Frau Kranki locks you out.'

'Well, yes, I . . . I do really . . .'

'Of course.' She prodded me on the nose. 'Well, why don't you go and have a nice bath and I'll make us a couple of drinks before you leave.'

'Yes . . .' I agreed readily, overwhelmed with relief at this avenue of escape.

'All right, you go on up.'

I staggered up the stairs, feet as heavy as a couple of anvils, turned on the bath taps, then, remembering my clothes were in her bedroom, went to get them.

As I was going along the landing, however, I heard the ding of the telephone bell down in the hall, then I heard her dialling a number. Intrigued, I stopped and listened, wondering who she could be calling.

When she spoke, her voice was deep, throaty seduction. 'Hi . . . it's me. You in bed? . . . Alone?' She chuckled sexily. 'What a criminal waste. Like to drop over for a nightcap? Ohhh . . . half an hour. Hm? I can't sleep. Ohh . . . the usual problem . . .' She chuckled again. 'Chuck, you *know* there's only one kind of pill that puts me to sleep. How're you feeling – all rested up?' She gave a tigerish growl. 'A whole week? You're kidding! Where have you been – in hospital? Hey, terrific . . . this *is* my lucky night. Well, we'll have to see what we can do to disperse all that disgusting energy. Half an hour? I'll be waiting . . .'

As she put down the receiver, I nipped into the bedroom for my clothes then returned to the bathroom and got into the bath, astounded at what I'd heard. She wanted more! Much more! She wanted a whole fresh fella!

I washed and dressed quickly, feeling safer with my clothes on, then went downstairs, relaxed in the knowledge that she'd want me off the premises pretty smartly if this 'Chuck' bloke was coming over.

She was lying on the sofa, dressed again in the satin robe, and smiling like she'd just come into money.

'Come and sit here,' she said, patting the sofa.

I sat very close to her, the sight of her lying there all languid and voluptuous, every curve and crevice plainly visible beneath the satin gown, starting my motor again despite everything I'd been through. She really was a cracking bird.

'Feeling better now?' she cooed, handing me my drink.

'Terrific,' I grinned. 'That bath really did the trick.'

She pouted. 'I should have been in it with you.'

'And how do you feel?'

With a reptilian grin her hand crept up my thigh and came to rest on Sleeping Beauty. 'How's my friend?'

My eyes lost focus as her legs slowly parted, taking the folds of the robe with them. 'He . . . he's waking up,' I gulped tremulously.

'So I can feel. Albert . . . ?' she said, her hands going to the sash of her gown.

'Yes, love?'

'One last time?'

I could only manage a nod.

'You beautiful man . . . get those silly clothes off.'

I never did get home that night.

I fell asleep over the wheel, parking the van.

CHAPTER NINE

Tuesday I put it in for her – the loft-ladder.

She was, due to Norman's presence, necessarily restrained, though she did manage a cheeky grab at one time while he was out at the van collecting the tools.

'How's my friend this morning?' she chuckled, giving him a tickle.

'I've booked him into the sanitorium for a rest cure.'

'Well, have him out by Saturday, whatever you do.'

'Oh?'

'I phoned Millie this morning, told her all about you. Darling, she's *ecstatic* at the prospect of a new face.'

'Face?' I grinned.

'You'll have a terrific time,' she promised. 'And I've told her she's got to introduce you to the girls from the estate, drum up some business for you.'

'That's awfully kind, Angela.'

'It's the least I can do in return for yesterday. I feel wonderful.'

'You certainly do,' I gulped, gnashing my teeth as Rod stirred from slumber at her touch.

'Oh, dear . . .' she sighed unhappily. 'What a pity we're not alone.'

'I c . . . could send Norman to Huddersfield for some screws?'

She shook her head. 'No, I have to go out now and I'll be out all day. You'll look after the house, I'm sure.'

'Of course.'

At the sound of Norman's return she moved away, suppressing a giggle as I struggled to re-arrange my entangled mate. 'I'll see you later, then. Anything you need – just help yourself.'

'And you,' I said and she burst out laughing as she went out of the door.

'What's up with her?' said Norman as she closed the front door.

'Oh . . . something tickled her. Right, let's get at it, we can finish this today.'

'What's the hurry, Albert?'

'I've got the feeling we're going to be rushed off our feet soon, old son. I think we're going to pick up quite a bit of business on this estate.'

'Oh? By recommendation, Albert?'

'Yeah,' I grinned. 'Something like that.'

We hadn't been going ten minutes when the phone rang. I scrambled down the ladder, ran downstairs and answered it.

'Is . . . Angela in?' a man asked hesitantly.

'No, she's out for the day.'

'Oh. Er, who's that?'

'I'm doing some work for her.'

'Oh.' He sounded relieved. 'Well, I'll call again. You might tell her Frank called, would you?'

'Frank – right.'

He rang off. I went back upstairs, climbed the ladder . . . and the bloody phone rang again.

'Hello?' I panted.

'Who's that?' a bloke demanded.

'I'm working here. Who's that?'

'Angela in?'

'No, she'll be out all day.'

'Fuck. Okay – tell her George called will you?'

'Roger.'

'No – George.'

'George – roger.'

'Smartarse,' he muttered and rang off.

This time I managed to get a pair of hinges on before it rang again.

' 'Ello!' I gasped, getting fed up with this.

'Who on earth is that?' queried a stockbroker voice.

'I'm working here. What can I do for you?'

'I wish to speak to Mrs. Lambert.'

'She'll be out all day. Any message?'

'No. Yes! Kindly tell her . . . her friend with the Rolls called.'

'Rolls. What kind – ham or cheese?' I chuckled.

'Don't be bloody insolent.'

He rang off.

'Busy phone,' remarked Norman as I rejoined him.

'Busy bird, mate,' I frowned, astounded anew by her prodigious capacity. Christ, just how many *did* she have in one day?

It was almost ten minutes before the phone rang again – and this time I thought I'd have a bit of fun. What the hell, she wouldn't miss one if he took umbrage.

'Mrs. Lambert's residence,' I announced pompously.

There was a short, shocked pause, then a deep, black man's voice rumbled, 'Hey, man, who the hell's that?'

'This is Mrs. Lambert's butler.'

His derisive laugh deafened me. 'Come off it, she ain't got no butler.'

'I started this morning.'

'Quit the crap an' put her on, whoever you are.'

'She'll be out all day. Who shall I say called?'

'Tell her Chuck phoned.'

'Oh, Chuck!' I exclaimed before I could stop myself.

There was another shocked pause. 'You *know* me? Hey, who is this?'

'I, er . . . I'm just working for Mrs Lambert. I'm putting in a loft-ladder.'

'So how come you know me?'

'I don't.'

'So what's all this "Oh, Chuck!" bit?'

'I, er . . .'

'And what's all this "butler" shit?'

'Well, I . . .'

'What the hell d'you think you're playin' at, man?'

I heaved a sigh. 'Chuck . . .'

'What?'

'Piss off.'

I put the phone down.

It rang immediately. 'Now, listen you . . . !'

'Who is calling, please?'

'It's CHUCK!'

'Oh, hi, Chuck, how's tricks?'

'I . . . I . . .' he stammered. 'Man, I am gonna come round and sort you *out*!'

'Sure, do that – there are only four of us.'

Crash! went the receiver.

'Who was that?' frowned Norman.

'Wrong number,' I told him.

The next call came just before lunch.

'MacFisheries!' I announced.

'*Who?*' laughed a tinkly female voice.

'Oh, er, Mrs. Lambert's residence.'

'Hoo hoo, very formal. And who might you be?'

Cor, what a voice – an alcohol rub with a mink glove.

'I'm Albert . . .'

'Albert!' she squealed excitedly. 'Oh, I've heard about you. This is Millie Armstrong! I believe you're coming to my party Saturday night.'

'Oh, hel*lo*, Mrs. Armstrong! Yes, I'd love to come. I'm looking forward to meeting you.'

'*Are* you now?' she cooed, slipping back into the bedroom husk. 'And I'm certainly looking forward to meeting you, too. Angela has told me *so* much about you.'

'Nothing good, I hope?'

'Nothing *but* good, Albert,' she laughed. 'She really is *very* impressed with your . . . your workmanship, can't praise it too highly, couldn't *wait* to pass on the good word to me, which is *marvellous* in these days of . . . I mean, good men are *so* hard to come by . . . oh, I'm *so* looking forward to it, Albert.'

The old ticker was thumping like a drum. 'That's . . . very nice to hear, Mrs. Armstrong. Er, what sort of . . . work did you have in mind for me?'

'Well, now, there are all *kinds* of little things you could do for me,' she replied, her tone teasingly suggestive. 'We have a very large house here and I'm sure I could find enough work to keep you here for simply ages . . . all *sorts* of interesting little things.'

'Wonderful,' I gulped. 'I shall look forward to getting down to them.'

She laughed uproariously.

'And . . . when would you like me to come, Mrs. Armstrong?'

Another bellow of laughter. 'Oh, *Al*bert . . . !'

'To the party, I mean.'

'Oh! Naughty me! Oh, come about ten o'clock, we'll be

nicely warmed up by then. I simply can't *stand* the first hour of a party.'

'Ten o'clock, fine. And thank you very much again.'

'It's *my* pleasure, Albert. Is Angela there?'

'No, she'll be out all day.'

'For the count, no doubt,' she growled sexily, then exploded with laughter again. 'All right, tell her I called, will you? Bye bye for now, Albert.'

'Toodle-oo, Mrs. Armstrong.'

She went out laughing.

By the cringe, another raver! And what incredible potential!

It was at that moment I decided I would like to be very rich – was *going* to be very rich! I'd been poor too long – and quite unnecessarily. It was now obvious that I had not, as the Americans would put it, been 'maximising my potential' – Millie Armstrong had just proven that. What a fool I'd been to waste my time, energy and talents painting and papering proletarian parlours when I could have been doing precisely the same thing up on Nob Hill – and for immensely greater reward!

Yes, from Saturday on, with Millie's help, I would select my clientele with perspicacity, would in future clear out only *rich* gutters, unblock only *well-to-do* drains – in short, up-market my entire enterprise. Yes, I could see it now – 'Albert Shifty Odd-Jobs Inc. – By Appointment to Her Maj . . .'

Well, perhaps that was going a *bit* far, still, we were now definitely on the right track.

'Al . . . bert!' wailed Norman from the loft.

'*What!*'

'I've got me fingers caught in the springs!'

Gawd, there was always something to bring you down to earth.

*   *   *

'Albert . . .'

'Yes, Norman.'

'You're putting that bracket in the wrong place.'

'Hm . . . ? Oh . . .'

'That's not like you, Albert.'

'No, it isn't.'

'Albert . . . you got somethin' on your mind?'

'Yes,' I sighed, downing tools and getting out my fags. 'Here – have a ciggy.'

'Not in any trouble, are yuh?' he asked, lighting up.

'Far from it, old comrade. Life could not be rosier than at this very moment.'

'So why the heavy brow?'

'Norman . . . there comes a time in every chap's life when he suddenly realises he's fed up with his old way of life.'

'And what are you tired of, Albert?'

'Pigging poverty.'

'Oh, that.'

'Yes – oh, that. Your rendering of the line illustrates my feelings on the matter precisely, for I, hitherto, have also dumbly accepted that virtual poverty is the condition in which I must fester for the rest of my life.'

'Nah, not you, Albert. You've got brains. You'll climb out of it sooner or later.'

'But much later than sooner, Norman, the way I've been going. It's very hard starting from absolute scratch. Somewhere along the line a bloke needs a leg up, a helping hand, a pointer to the short-cut. It takes a rotten life-time to go the long way round.'

'Wishin' is one thing, finding it's another, though, Albert.'

'Yes, Norman,' I said quietly. 'But I think I've found it.'

'I mean, you . . . hm?' he stared at me.

'I said, mate, I think I've found it.'

His eyes widened. 'Get away! Eh, nuthin' illegal, is it?'

I laughed. 'No, not illegal. A touch immoral, maybe, but nobody will get hurt. Come to think of it, a lot of people may get very happy. Well, certainly happier than they are at the moment.'

'Go on,' he gaped. 'What have you found?'

I drew on my cigarette and blew smoke at the rafters. 'I've been invited to a party Saturday night. Big house in Kingston. Very rich people . . . and a very bored wife.'

It took a moment for it to sink in, then a grin split his face. 'Blimey! And how did *you* cop an invitation?'

'Through Mrs. Lambert. These rich people used to live on this estate and they still keep in touch with their old mates, throw them a party every now and then . . . like this Saturday night. And yours truly is going to be there.'

'Blimey,' he gasped again. 'What an opportunity!'

I nodded. 'Think of all those big rich houses up on Nob Hill.'

'I'm thinkin'! I'm thinkin'!'

'We could be in there, Norman – catering to the cream.'

'Yers! Oooh, Albert, it gives me the shivers. Hee hee . . . !' he cheered, fetching the ladder bracket a thump with the hammer. 'I can see us now – drivin' to work in a golden Rolls Royce . . . knockin' off for lunch at the Ritz!'

'This could be the start of a whole new life for us, Norman.'

'Provided you come up trumps with the wife, Albert?'

'Yes – provided I do that, old friend.'

'Hey, you've got to get lots of rest . . . take the rest of the week off, I'll do all the work.' He lapsed into fantastic reverie, clearly seeing our new, exciting future. 'Just fancy . . . knocking off for lunch at the Ritz.'

'Which reminds me,' I said, glancing at my watch. 'It's one o'clock – time for a burger at the Wimpey.'

He curled his lip. 'Aw, rotten heck. Roll on bleedin' Saturday.'

'Yes,' I grinned. 'Roll on Saturday.'

CHAPTER TEN

Saturday did indeed roll on, though crawl was more like it, and nine p.m. saw me putting the final touches to an ensemble which, with all modesty, could only be described as devastating.

Knowing that first impressions would be vital, I had blown a month's earnings on a Cecil Gee suit of dark green velvet, a swiss lawn shirt in patterned primrose yellow, a green silk tie, and a pair of tan Italian shoes that were so comfy I kept looking down to make sure I'd still got them on.

Freshly bathed, closely shaved, and smelling like a West End barber shop, I tucked a matching lawn hanky into my breast pocket and was ready for the off.

Cautiously opening the door, I peered out, saw the coast was clear and started down the stairs, not at all anxious to attract the attention of the inmates who I knew would bombard me with an avalanche of stupid comment.

I got no further than the first stair.

'Hey, Albert . . . !' exclaimed Norman behind me. 'Hey . . . wow! . . . oh, boy! . . . terrific . . . !'

I turned, sheepishly. 'Thank you, Norman.'

'No, hey, I mean it! You look fantastic! Where did you nick the whistle?'

'C.G.'s.'

'Crikey, must've set you back a fortune!'

'An investment, old chum – a sprat to catch a mackerel.'

'Damn right,' he grinned. 'You deserve a whale with that kind of clobber.'

'Ta, son. I shall certainly do my best.'

'I'll be rootin' for you, Albert. Best of luck.'

'Thanks.' I started down the stairs. 'If I don't get back – you can have the van!'

As I hit the lower landing, Peter's door flew open and his head popped out, eyes growing into saucers. 'Oooooh, *Albert* . . . !' he gasped, and I thought he was going to swoon.

'Oh, what a *gorg*eous suit! And the *shirt* . . . ! And *every-*thing . . . ! Oooh, I've gone goosebumps all over.'

'Thanks, Peter,' I grinned, racing on.

'*Do* tell me where you got them!'

'C.G.'s – Shaftesbury Avenue! Ask for Cyril – he's the one with the warm tape-measure!'

On the third landing I almost collided with Bennie, coming out of the bathroom. 'Christ . . . it's Beau Brummel! Hey, baby, I *dig* dose threads!'

'Ta, Bennie . . .'

'Bang goes another virginity!'

'I'm banking on it!'

Jesus, now Harriet Bloom's door was opening.

'Oh, my God . . . !' she gasped, dramatically clutching her bosom and collapsing against the doorpost.

'Like it!' I grinned, doing a twirl for her.

'Love it! Just *love* it! Oh, if only I was twenty years youn-ger – *and* ten stone lighter. That poor girl, she won't know what hit her.'

'Wanna bet?' grinned Bennie.

'Shut your crude mouth, Bennie Kenton, sex isn't every-thing, you know.'

'What else can there be?' he frowned.

'Romance, you randy sod. Aesthetic beauty. You don't know what beautiful clothes mean to a girl.'

'Then how come my bird can never wait to tear mine off?' he cracked, winking at me.

'Because you always turn up in your bus uniform!' she retorted.

I continued on down the stairs.

'Good huntin', Albert!' Bennie shouted over the bannister. 'Shoot one for me!'

I managed to negotiate the second landing without further interruption, but then ran smack into Dillys on the ground floor, looking particularly exotic in hair curlers and a new nylon blouse.

'Ohhhh . . . !' she gasped, her hands instinctively flying up to hide her curlers. 'Oh, Albert, you *do* look nice.'

'Thanks, Dillys, so do you,' I said, ogling her charlies. 'Lovely blouse.'

She preened bashfully. 'Do you really like it?'

'They're . . . it's a knockout, love. Really does something for you.'

'So does your suit, Albert, I think it's smashing. You . . . got a date, then?'

'No, just a party.'

'I wish I was going with you.'

'So do I,' I lied.

'Albert . . . do you mind if I touch it?'

'Hm? Oh, the suit!' I grinned. 'No, go on, help yourself.'

Tentatively she reached out and ran her fingers down my sleeve, shivering at the sensation. 'It's gorgeous!' she giggled. 'But I bet the trousers feel even nicer.'

'Now, Dillys . . .'

She took a step closer. 'Oh, Albert, it's been so long . . .'

'Yes, love, yes . . . we'll work something out. But I've got to fly now, I'll be late.'

'All right. Have a lovely time.'

'Thanks, angel.'

'And be good! Save it for me!'

'Right!'

I ran down the front steps to the van.

How bloody ignominious – a million dollar outfit and ten cent transportation. It just wasn't right. I should have been stepping into a Porche Turbo Coupe or a Lamborghini Espada. Well, never mind, that would come. Tonight I'd hide the old wreck in a nearby thicket and walk the last hundred yards to the house.

I started the engine and drove off, bubbling inside like a spoonful of Enos in a glass of water. Yaaaahooo! I felt good. Right, world, this is where you get yours. Stand back, everybody, Shifty is coming through! – straight to the top!

Yes, I could see it now . . . the Shifty mansion, on the very crest of Nob Hill – a long, low Spanish-type villa with flower-filled courtyards and tinkling fountains, set in a square mile of landscaped gardens so beautiful they'd make Hampton Court's look like a bomb crater.

That's the Shifty place, you know, they'd say in passing . . . my word, he *has* done well. Can you believe that only two years ago he was living in an attic in Frau Kranki's boarding house? How did he do it? Well, they *do* say . . . snigger, snigger . . .

Screw 'em all, I wouldn't care what they said. It was the end that mattered, not the means. I'd had a bellyful of grot and poverty, of Frau Kranki's rotten cooking and rotting room, and if pleasuring the frustrated missus of a rich, fat barrow-boy was the means – she was damn-well going to get it in the end!

Thus determined, I roared up Putney High Street and onto the Kingston By-pass, impatient to begin.

Ha!

What a blessing – or is it a curse? – that we are denied sight of even our immediate future. Because if I'd known at that moment what lay ahead for me in the world of the rich . . . I'd have turned right round and driven like hell in the opposite direction!

CHAPTER ELEVEN

Ten minutes later I turned off the dual carriageway onto the approach road which leads up to Nob Hill. A few minutes more and the roar of the highway gave way to the kind of sedate, blue-chip silence you find only in the best British stockbroker belts, along avenues of manicured grass verges, well-bred specimen trees, and splendid houses almost concealed from the road by high and haughty hedges.

Geographically primed by Angela Lambert, I located *Long Acre* without trouble and drove slowly past, my heart lurching at its splendour. It was a vast two-storey Neo-Georgian job in pale yellow brick, approached by a curving tarmac drive and fronted by magnificent lawns and flower-beds, set well back from the road behind tall, ornate wrought-iron gates and a ten-foot laurel hedge.

The light blazing from umpteen windows made the place look cozy and inviting, and I couldn't wait to dump the van in the nearest shadow and get in there.

I parked it and walked back, nerves tingling and stomach in knots, wondering how it would go. I couldn't believe it was happening to *me*. Albert Shifty hob-nobbing with the dudes – my father would have died laughing.

As I reached the gates a uniformed figure, on the other side of them, came out of the shadows and confronted me, his eyes raking me suspiciously. 'Yes, sir?'

'My name's Shifty. I'm a guest of Mrs. Armstrong.'

He consulted a clip-board. 'Shufty?'

'No . . . Shifty.'

'Hang on, I'll have a shufty,' he laughed, cheeky bastard. 'Oh, yers, here we are . . . Albert Shifty, right at the bottom.'

Tucking the board under his arm, he used both hands to open one half of the gates and let me in. 'You, er, on foot, sir?' he enquired with surprise.

'Er, yes . . . I only live down the road. It's such a beautiful night I thought I'd walk.'

'Yes . . . beautiful,' he sniffed, throwing a glance at the moon and the clear, starlit sky. 'Lovely night for a swim.'

'Oh, swimming, are they?'

'They're doin' everything – as usual. Your first time here, sir?'

'Yes, first time.'

'Well, you'll find all the goings on going on round the pool at the back. Go through that side-gate in the wall there, it'll save you going through the house.'

'Thank you. Many here, are there?'

'Ohh . . . fifty or sixty, usual crowd. There'll be more later on, no doubt. Have a nice time, sir.'

'Thanks.'

As I started up the long drive I gave my imagination free reign, imagined this was all mine and that I was just coming home from the office. What an incredible feeling. I'd open the front door with my key and there in the hall would be a cracking bird in a sexy Paris gown, waiting to greet me with a long cool drink and hot puckered lips.

'Albie, baby . . . didums have a hard day, then? Come to momma and she'll make it all better for you.'

Ah, yes, I think I could adapt without too much bother.

I reached the wrought-iron gate in the wall and through it could see an immense garden, stretching so far back that the end of it was lost in darkness. The house was inaccurately named, it should have been Long Ten Acres. Then again, maybe it was their little joke.

Off to my left was a large tarmac-ed area filled with cars, mostly modest down-market models – presumably belonging to the Belview crowd – but here and there the odd Jaguar or Mercedes lurked in snooty splendour, pretending they weren't with the plebian heaps.

It'd serve you right if I brought my van in, I thought. That'd give you something to snoot about.

I opened the gate and went through, ventured down the side of the house, slowing as I reached the rear corner, and there, from the shadows, I popped my head round to see what I was walking into.

Oh, boy . . . what a sight. It was like a set from a James Bond movie.

Across the entire width of the house ran a wide patio bedecked with gay umbrella-ed tables and lit by lanterns and fairy lights strung between shady trees. In its centre was a terrazzo dance floor on which twenty couples were Frugging themselves into a stupor to music coming from loudspeakers suspended in the trees. And on the far right of the patio – a long stone-built bar, a raised barbecue pit attended by two uniformed chefs, and half a dozen trestle-tables laden with food.

Further right still was the fabulous swimming pool, a huge, magnificently landscaped affair, big enough and deep enough to warrant a twenty-foot diving tower.

What a place! And all from one swift, under-the-armpit deal in scrap metal. Shifty, I thought, you're going about it all the wrong way, lad. You should be *collecting* loft-ladders, not installing them.

Well, I couldn't stand there gawping all night, I had to get in there and set the ball rolling. So, drawing a deep breath to steady my twanging nerves, I took a bold step forward and sauntered into the melee as though I owned the joint.

Within a few strides the living room came into view – an immense and breathtakingly beautiful lounge, its glass doors open to the patio, filled with antiques, crystal chandeliers, flock wallpaper, lush carpets, satin-covered suites – and another gaggle of guests, all standing around drinking, smoking, laughing, talking and making a terrific din, a noise I found most consoling.

I continued on, making an unhurried bee-line for the bar, feeling the need of a good stiff Dutch Courage and tonic.

The barman was a tubby, friendly soul – and why shouldn't he be, he wasn't paying for all this.

'Good evenin', sir,' he bid me cordially. 'And what might your fancy be?'

'The blonde in the red cat-suit,' I said, turning for another eyeful of her incredible bottom twitching like a windscreen wiper, out on the dance-floor.

'Sir has impeccable taste,' he chuckled, then, feeling he was among friends, reverted to his native Cockney. 'Bin smackin' me lips over that one for the past ten minutes. Lovely bit of duff, that. But what else can I do for you, sir?'

'Vodka tonic?'

'Yours for the arskin'.'

Deftly, showing off a bit in fact, he poured half a pint of vodka into a tall glass from a great height, then added a toothful of tonic for the sake of appearances.

'There you go, cock . . . sir . . . that'll send you down the runway.'

'Cheers.'

I took a gulp and coughed.

'More tonic, sir?'

I shook my head. 'There's no room.'

I turned to survey the gay, flamboyant scene, sizing up the birds in one deadly hawk-like swoop, then came back slowly for a more leisurely appraisal. Not a bad bunch at all – with one or two real breath-stoppers.

'You . . . doin' a solo, sir?' enquired the barman, obviously encouraged to such familiarities by the Belview crowd.

'Yes, I am.'

'Bin here before, sir?' he continued, unhygienically huffing on a glass to polish it.

'No, I haven't.'

'Thought I hadn't seen you before. I'd have remembered.'

'Oh?' I turned to him, flattered by the compliment – or perhaps it wasn't. 'You work here often, I take it.'

'Haven't missed a single wing-ding since the boss bought this place two years ago. Blimey . . .' he shook his head, '. . . he certainly knows how to throw a party. They really enjoy themselves, do the Belview crowd. Drink? They sink enough to float the Ark Royal.'

'They seem sober enough at the moment.'

'Give 'em time, sir, they haven't got their second wind yet. You from Belview, are you?'

'No.'

'Oh, so you don't know many of them?'

'No. I only know one lady, the one who got me the invitation, and I can't see her around at the moment.'

'Ah – so that means they don't know you, either,' he persisted, and I could tell something was coming.

'That's right.'

'Ho ho . . .' he laughed suggestively. 'Then I'd certainly like to be in your shoes.'

I frowned at him. 'Why?'

He slid me a filthy leer. 'What – a good-lookin' bloke like you! I should cocoa. Wait till these birds clap eyes on you *and* find you're unattached – you'll more than likely be killed in the rush!'

I frowned on, playing dumb, wanting to hear the words, excited by this confirmation of what I'd already heard. 'I'm sorry, I'm not with you . . .'

His eyes widened. 'You mean you haven't heard? Blimey, I thought everyone had heard of the goings on in Belview! Ho, a right lot of little swingers, this mob. Their motto is "do what the 'ell you like provided it's with someone else's husband or missus".' He roared with laughter. 'Cor, the things they get up . . . blue movies, wife-swappin', car-key parties . . .'

'Really! No, I hadn't heard, I've only just moved into the district.'

'Lucky you!' he chortled, taking a drag of his fag and exploding into a coughing fit. 'Oooh, I must give these up, they're killin' me. So – how did you get the invite tonight, then?'

None of your bloody business, I thought.

'Mrs. Armstrong's a friend of my mother's,' I told him, and that sobered him.

'Oh . . .' he said lamely, and didn't have a chance to say any more because at that moment a group of six people, three men, three women, left the dance floor and came over, laughing uproariously.

'Right, Jack, me old mate!' called out a small, bald fellow, smacking his hands together, 'let's be havin' yuh! Drinkies all round for six thirsty Fruggers!'

'What'll it be, Mister Penfold?' beamed Jack sycophantically.

While Penfold gathered in the orders, I was inspecting the women. Two of them were blondes, one with short hair, the other long, and the third girl was a dyed red-head with enormous knockers. They were all dressed in short summer dresses and not at all a bad-looking trio, all young – in their twenties – and nicely put together.

The red-head spotted me first.

In the middle of a laugh at something Penfold said, she caught sight of me from the corner of her eye and her head snapped round so fast she almost broke her neck.

Zing!

Our eyes collided . . . and for a short sizzling eternity remained spot-welded together. Then, with a cheeky smile and a blatant head-to-toe appraisal, she turned away and surreptitiously muttered something to her friend with the long blonde hair.

Round came the blonde for an eyeful, her eyes dancing mischievously, their playful sexiness catching me a blow under the heart.

While all this was going on, the red-head had moved closer to the blonde with the short hair and was relaying the news to her . . . and now *she* pirouetted for a butcher's. And now all three of them were at it, grinning and murmuring and nudging one another as though they'd just spotted a bloke with his dick hanging out.

'Here y'are, Liz . . .' said Penrose, handing a drink to the red-head. 'A gin for you, Beryl . . .' he said to the short-haired blonde, '. . . and a scotch for Rita.'

'Ta, Syd,' said the long-haired blonde. 'Cheers.'

Taking a drink, she gave me the eyes over the rim, a naughty, collusive grin that told me her flag was up and flying.

Penrose sank half his scotch and belched disgustingly. 'Cor, that's better. 'Ere, let's sit down and have a breather, I'm Frugged to a stan'still.'

They wandered off across the patio to a vacant table, the girls sending back secret smiles of coquettish interest as they sat down.

'See what I mean?' chortled Jack behind me. 'They're ga-ga for you, mate. I reckon you're gonna do yourself a bit of good tonight.'

And not only tonight, I thought, heart thumping with excitement. How about the future! There were three potential loftladders for starters! By heaven, it was going to work!

*   *   *

Time passed.

The crowd flowed and ebbed, milled and surged, out of the house and on to the dance-floor, around the barbecue stand and the food tables – and particularly to the bar, so much so that

Jack finally had to call in two of the food waiters to help serve the drinks.

I stayed close to the bar because I felt more comfortable there – and it was also the best place from which to study the menagerie.

Things were bubbling along a treat now, everybody nicely high and very relaxed, the furor punctuated every now and then by a shriek of female laughter – always an accurate gauge of the success of any party.

Well, I was standing there, enjoying an eyeful of knickers from a bird who'd just fallen flat on her back while attempting to Limbo under a broom handle held by two men, when a softly whispered, 'Hi . . .' crept into my right ear and blew my brains out.

I spun round, my pulse exploding as I came nose-to-nose with the hugely-knockered red-head . . . What the hell was her name? . . . Liz!

'Oh . . . hi,' I smiled, my eyes plummeting down her cleavage before I could stop them.

She smiled warmly, not minding at all. 'I think it's a crime – you standing here all this time all alone. A *terrible* waste. You ought to be ashamed of yourself, denying us girls the pleasure.'

I grinned, bashfully. They like that. 'Well, that's very nice of you . . . "Liz", isn't it?'

She frowned with surprise, then the smile came . . . like the slow burn of a high-explosive fuse. 'Hey . . . you're cute. You heard it *and* remembered.'

'I have a good memory . . . for things that interest me.'

'Zow . . . *eee*,' she murmured, eyes dancing. 'Are *you* something . . . *and* brand new.' Her eyes went to the dance-floor. 'Would you like to?'

I nodded, heart banging, tingling at the prospect of being squashed against those breasts.

She led off, I followed. She made for the centre of the crowd, then turned and slid into me, everything hitting me at once – breasts, belly, crutch, thighs, her mouth up close to my ear.

'Nice,' she husked sexily. 'So go ahead – tell me.'

'Tell you what?'

'Who? Why? When? What? How! The girls are going *mad*

134

with curiosity. You're the dishiest thing that's happened around here in months.'

'Oh?' I laughed.

'"Oh" he says. He's got every bird in the place panting with curiosity and all he says is "oh".' She looked up at me, slack-mouthed, inviting, so close I could smell the perfume of her lipstick. 'What's your name?'

'Albert.'

'Terrific. Don't tell me you live on Belview, I won't believe it.'

'No, I live in Fulham.'

'So how did you get here?'

'I . . . did some work for a lady – two ladies in fact – who live on Belview. I installed loft-ladders for them.'

'Oh? And who were they?'

'A Mrs. Pinkerton and a Mrs. Lambert.'

She stopped dancing, regarded me with a mocking grin, then got back to it, cuddling even closer. 'Well, now . . .'

'You know them?'

She gave a little wry laugh. 'Yes, I know them. Which one got you the invitation – Lambert?'

'Yes, as a matter of f . . .'

'It figures. She's a close friend of Millie Armstrong. Tell me, have you met your hostess yet . . . no, no need to answer, it's obvious you haven't or you wouldn't have been standing around spare.'

'Oh? What would I be doing?'

She cocked a brow at me. 'Come on, you're not that naive. Come to think of it, you're not naive at all – you know the score. If you've worked for both Vickie Pinkerton and Angela Lambert you most certainly know the score.' She gave me a grin. 'You may have gone into Angie's house a virgin, but no way would you have come out intact.'

I said nothing, just smiled enigmatically.

'You're not *saying* very much, Albert,' she teased.

'My lips are sealed – professional etiquette.'

She exploded a laugh. 'I like that – the strong *and* silent type. Is there no end to your virtues, Albert?' She snuggled back into my neck. 'So . . . Angie was *so* delighted with your . . .

135

handywork . . . that she recommended you to Millie, is that right?'

'I believe that's how it was, yes.'

'You must be *very* good, Albert,' she cooed, teasing her fingers into my neck hair.

'I'm like Avis car rentals,' I grinned. 'I try harder.'

She chuckled warmly in my ear. 'Do you, now. Hmm . . . that deserves a little thought.'

We fell to silence.

A moment later she began working on me, a little extra thigh pressure, a belly caress, her fingers kneading my neck. And hearing reveille, old Rodders pricked up his ears, stretched, yawned, and began doing push-ups, drawing a stifled gasp from her as he made his presence felt.

'Hey . . . that's naughty! We've only just been introduced.'

'Strange . . . I feel we're old friends already.'

'Do you . . . oops!'

Using a slight collision from the rear, she thrust her pubic hummock into him, gasping again at the contact. 'Wow . . . you're right, you *do* try harder.'

Maintaining our new-found contact, we danced on, her breathing now disrupted, loud in my ear. Suddenly, with a moan, she broke away, gasping, 'Christ . . .' her eyes startled.

I grinned. 'What's the matter?'

She didn't answer. A moment later she eased back again, whispering urgently, 'Listen . . . how much do you charge for your damned loft-ladders?'

My heart leapt. 'A . . . hundred and twenty pounds.'

'What! I meant the ladder – not a new loft.'

I shrugged helplessly. 'They're made of aluminium . . . it's expensive. And there's a lot of work involved. I have to make a new hatch-cover and . . .'

She wasn't listening. She raised her cheek from my neck and gave me a *very* sexy grin. 'How about after-sales service?'

'As long as you want – all you have to do is call.'

She nodded. 'I'll have one.'

I stared at her. 'Hm . . . ?'

'I *said* . . . I'll have one.'

'A . . . a ladder?'

She laughed at my expression. 'Well, of *course* a ladder!'

'Oh, boy . . . well, thank you very much! Er, when would you . . .'

'How about Monday?'

'Yes, Monday's fine, I've got nothing on.'

She gave me one hell of a grin. 'Keep it that way. Come round at eleven o'clock. I live at number two-six-four. Don't *dare* forget it.'

'You think I would – or could? Here . . .' I reached into my pocket and took out a business card. 'Call me if . . . you have to change the time or anything.'

She tucked the card down her cleavage, smiling to herself. 'You've really got it down to a fine art, haven't you?'

'That'll be for you to say.'

She was about to reply, but her eyes went over my shoulder. 'Oh, the conniving bitch . . .'

'Who?'

'Rita – my pal with the long blonde hair. You *do* remember Rita?'

'No,' I lied.

'Liar,' she grinned.

'What about her?'

'She is *very* sneakily heading this way . . . dragging the slob she's dancing with in this direction. She's dying to dance with you.'

'Oh?' I gulped, choked with excitement.

'She's lovely really. I may do her a big favour and let her have a go.'

'That's surprisingly generous of you.'

'No, I'm on safe ground – she's already *got* a loft-ladder. Here she comes . . . stand by for a great performance.'

'Well, hell*o*!' exclaimed Rita, behind me. 'If it isn't Lizzie . . . fancy meeting you here.'

Liz turned me round to greet her.

Rita, an extremely haveable little piece with nice green eyes and shiny hair, batted her eyelashes at me, then transferred to Liz, pretending she'd come over to gossip about who was there.

The chap she was dancing with – a thin-faced individual who looked like a window-cleaner – was swaying drunk and looked in danger of falling flat on his face any second.

'Who's your friend?' murmured Liz, nodding at him.

Rita shrugged, then flashed a look at me. 'Who's yours?'

'Mine's lovely.'

Rita stuck out her hand. 'Hello, lovely, I'm Rita.'

I took it. 'I'm really Albert.'

'Fantastic. Where did you pop up from, thank God?'

'Leave him alone, he's already spoken for,' warned Liz. 'He's going to put a loft-ladder in for me.'

Rita's eyes grew big. 'You're in loft-ladders?'

'Among other things. I hear you already have one?'

'Yes, dammit.'

'Then perhaps I could interest you in something else?'

'Without a shadow of a doubt,' she growled.

'Hey, you two . . .' muttered Liz.

Rita turned on her. 'Liz, dear, did you know this was a Ladies' Excuse Me? Here . . .' she held out her biffed partner's hand, '. . . cop hold of this. Feed him twice a day and don't get too close to the bars.'

'I hope your rabbits die,' sneered Liz, winking at me. 'I'll be *seeing* you. Come on, handsome, let's waltz you back to the bar . . .'

As they disappeared, Rita rounded on me with a swift full-Nelson. 'Now . . . tell me all about your lovely loft-ladders . . . I just *adore* that suit. *Very* sexy.'

'Thank you.'

She released a sigh. '*How* come you're here all alone, Albert? I mean, it's just un*true*!'

I told her the story, and watched a succession of reactions, thoughts, plots, plans and wicked intrigues parade across her countenance during the telling. This was a *very* naughty lady.

'Pity you already have a loft-ladder,' I sighed. 'But how about a bit of flooring in the attic to go with it?'

She pulled a miserable face. 'It's already in.'

'Oh. Then . . . how about a bit of decorating?'

'It's just been decorated – right through.'

'Oh. Well, how about . . .'

She scalded me with a lascivious leer. 'How about forgetting the damned excuses and just come and see me?' she said forthrightly. 'Number two-eight-two. I make a great cup of coffee.'

'Fantastic,' I grinned.

'How about Wednesday afternoon?'

'How about that.'

'Come to think of it . . . there *is* a job you can do for me . . .'

'Oh?'

'I want a shelf put in a built-in wardrobe . . .'

'Fine.'

'. . . in my bedroom.'

I coughed.

She studied me, smilingly. 'If this keeps up, you'll be a wealthy man. Six hundred houses on the estate . . .'

'Oh, I think it's unlikely I'd get a job in every one of them, don't you?'

She gave a shrug. 'Oh, I don't know. I reckon Liz and I could get you at least a dozen jobs . . .'

'Really! Hey, that would be marvellous!'

'*Provided*, of course . . .' her eyes crinkled, '. . . that you did a terrific job for us.'

'Oh, of course.'

'I mean, we could hardly recommend you if *we* weren't well-satisfied, now could we?'

'Oh . . . absolutely not.'

'So . . .' she shrugged, tilting her head coquettishly, 'it's up to you.'

CHAPTER TWELVE

Funny how dreams and longings can suddenly, out of the blue, come true. One minute you're dawdling along as you've always dawdled, steeped in the wishful thinking that over the years has become as much a habit as breathing, without any real hope or prospect of things changing for the better, then suddenly – woomf! A totally unexpected avenue of possibility opens up to you.

Opportunity – in the form of Vickie Pinkerton's phone call – had, I now knew, knocked on Albert Shifty's door. Its second knock had come through Angela Lambert's friendship with Millie Armstrong . . . which had got me the invitation to the party . . . which had already landed me a job with Liz and Rita . . . who were promising to recommend me to others . . . and suddenly the erstwhile hope of doing a job for every one of the six hundred houses on Belview loomed as a distinct and wildly exciting possibility!

Alone once again, I stood at the end of the bar, casually watching the crowd but thinking intently about business, about money, about all the incredible potential that lay dormant in Belview.

Six hundred houses . . . six hundred loft-ladders at one hundred and twenty five pounds each was . . . I was too tiddly for mental arithmetic, so I dipped a finger into my drink and traced the sum on the bar . . . was . . . an unbelievable *seventy five thousand quid*!

A flaming fortune!

Okay . . . okay, calm down, you can forget six hundred for a start! Not everybody's going to be able to afford a hundred and twenty five quid for a ladder. *But* . . . say I only did *ten percent* of the houses! It was still a fortune – seven thousand five hundred pounds!

Sixty houses – not much to ask for! I'd got three already – Angela, Vickie and Liz – with Liz's and Rita's connections to come. Rita had said that she and Liz could come up with a dozen contacts – now say each of *those* women came up with

a dozen! That'd be ... it was back to the bar counter again ...
a hundred and forty four plus the original twelve ... a hundred
and fifty six ... times a hundred and twenty five pounds ...

My concentration was suddenly shattered by a shriek of
female laughter. I looked round. Into the crowd came a dapper
little woman, in her thirties, a plump little bird with curly-
blonde hair, wearing an expensive ankle-length red dress and
more diamonds than the Queen Mum on gala night.

With her she brought a cluster of laughing friends, all tiddly
and looking for more.

'Jack ... !' she hailed the barman. 'Champers for this lot –
I'll have a Millie Special!'

'Coming right up, Mrs. Armstrong!'

So – this was the infamous Millie ... and a right character
she looked, too. Brash, flashy, but fun – and obviously having a
whale of a time at her own party.

I enjoyed watching her, found myself grinning at her antics
and laughing at her jokes.

Then suddenly, by chance, during a rowdy exchange of
banter, her eyes swept across me, travelled on, then shot back
again. For a moment she frowned at me, blankly, her expression questioning 'who the heck are you?', then, with a puzzled
shake of her head she returned to the fray.

Several times during the next few minutes she chanced a
glance, at first still puzzled, thoughtful, but suddenly with a
flash of awareness. With a smile to me that told me she'd
solved the puzzle, she continued with the banter, sending me
only one further look that said 'careful – don't call me, I'll call
you'.

I turned away but continued watching her from the corner
of my eye. Subtly, so gradually no one could have noticed,
she eased in my direction, chattering all the time, until finally
she was standing right behind me. Then, as though turning
quickly to order another drink, she whirled and caught my arm
with her near-empty glass.

'Ohhh ... !' she exclaimed. 'Oh, I'm so sorry, did I splash
your suit?'

'No, no damage done – just a broken arm,' I grinned.

'Jack! Something for a broken arm!'

'One splint – coming up!'

'I don't think we've met,' she said, holding out her hand. 'I'm Millie.'

'I'm Albert.'

She nodded. 'Of course. Got a drink?'

I held up my glass. 'Nine parts vodka, one part tonic.'

She shrugged. 'How else would you drink it? Excuse me . . .' she leaned past me, collected a fresh drink from Jack. 'Well, cheers . . . very glad you could come.'

'So am I. I haven't seen any sign of Angela.'

She shook her head, eyes twinkling at me. 'She couldn't make it. She's developed a bit of a temperature. She's flat on her back, poor thing.'

'Oh, I am sorry. Under the doctor, is she?'

She roared with laughter. 'Oh, I like you. Hey, do you dance?'

'Opinions vary.'

'Come on – I'll give you mine.'

We threaded our way into the crowd and began dancing, at first separately, keeping a respectable distance, just going with the music.

'So, she smiled, 'how's the loft-ladder business?'

'Oh . . . up and down.'

She exploded with laughter again. 'You kill me! Angie tells me you could do with a little help.'

I shrugged. 'All contributions would be gratefully received right now.'

'Broke?'

'No, not stoney.'

'At least you spend it well. I *love* your suit. You didn't by chance buy it specially for tonight, did you?'

I grinned.

'Sweet,' she nodded. 'You look *very* handsome, Albert.'

Suddenly the music changed to something slow and sexy.

'Thank God for that,' she muttered, coming into me, running her hands over my suit as she slid them round to hold me close. 'Hey, that feels *good*.'

She wriggled closer, filling nook and cranny, letting me know she was built for comfort. 'Comfy?'

'Wonderful.'

'I can feel your heart pounding.'

'Me, too,' I laughed. 'It seems to have been doing quite a bit of that lately.'

'So I heard,' she chuckled. 'I believe you won six gold medals in some kind of Olympics.'

'An exaggeration, Millie. It was only five.'

'Want to *try* for six?' she murmured in my ear.

'Lead me to the starting blocks.'

She chuckled throatily. 'Precisely what I had in mind.'

We smooched on, barely moving on the packed floor, unaware of anything that was going on around us as we worked on each other. By the end of the second number she was practically inside my trousers.

'Albert . . .' she moaned softly.

'Yes, Millie?'

'Don't you find it offensively crowded around here?'

'Offensively,' I nodded.

'There's a place I'd like to show you.'

'Oh? Where is it?'

'*Way* down at the bottom of the garden. It's my little hidey-hole . . . a summer house. When things get too hectic up here I slip away into the darkness and disappear for an hour. I find it *very* soothing.'

'Sounds terrific.'

'You'd love it. It's very cozy. It has a bar . . . and music . . . and a huge water bed . . .'

'Really?' I gulped.

'Have you ever lain on a water bed, Albert?'

'No, I haven't.'

She laughed, deep and low. 'You haven't lived. They're incredible . . . unbe*liev*ably comfortable. You really ought to try it.'

'I'd . . . love to, Millie. But when?'

'Oh . . . later on.' She looked around her, at the crowd. 'Give them another hour and they won't know *who* their hostess is, never mind where she is. Leave it to me, I'll let you know.'

'All right.'

She smiled up at me, her eyes warm, excited, her fingers probing the muscles in my back. '*Gor*geous . . .'

'The suit?' I grinned.

'The man,' she growled.

143

Suddenly her eyes darted to my left, and with a change of expression she eased away from me, saying, under cover of a frothy laugh, 'My dear husband has just come out of the house and he's got his beady eye on me.'

My heart plummeted. 'Oh . . .' I threw a glance towards the house. 'Which one is he?'

'The one who looks as though he's about to explode all over the patio.'

He wasn't difficult to recognise. It was Frank Cannon with hair, Mister Michelin who'd been left on the air-hose too long. He was enormous! Belly on him like a weather balloon, fat hanging everywhere like melted wax.

'Fine figure of a man,' I observed.

'Fine figure of three men,' she retorted. 'Come on, I'd better introduce you or he *will* get suspicious.'

'Oh?' I croaked. 'Bit touchy, is he?'

'Wouldn't you be if you looked like him and he looked like you?'

As we made our way over, Angela Lambert's observation about Freddie Armstrong's sex problem – and therefore Millie's – came back to me. How could he *do* it with a belly on him like a truck bumper? He'd need a dong three feet long just to clear the overhang! No wonder Millie got it where she could.

The closer we got, the more gross Freddie became. Wearing dark blue slacks and a multi-hued Hawaiian-type shirt, in close-up he resembled a walking Picasso mural – a vast blast of colour atop two skinny legs.

As I drew up, his dark brown eyes – two pin-pricks in a blob of dough – held me with cool, suspicious disdain, his lip curled as he took in my appearance . . . height, weight, hair, age and suit. And under this cold, unfriendly appraisal my blood froze. The game was up. Freddie Armstrong was already on to me!

'Hi . . . !' Millie greeted him, over-jovial to allay suspicion. 'Freddie, dear, I'd like you to meet a very good friend of Angela Lambert's. This is Albert . . .' she faltered, not knowing my surname.

'Shifty,' I grinned, extending my hand. 'Very pleased to meet you, Mister Armstrong.'

'How are yuh,' he grunted, broad Cockney, and covered my

puny mitt with his polar bear's paw. 'Oh, Angela's here, is she?'

'Well . . . no . . .' I faltered. 'No, actually . . . she went down with a bit of a temperature tonight . . .'

'Oh, yers? So you came along on your own, did you?'

'Well . . . yes . . .'

Millie leapt in. 'Angela phoned me and asked me if it'd be all right, Freddie. Albert's been doing some work for her and she thinks so highly of him, she wants me to introduce him to some of the Belview people, see if we can get him some work.'

'Oh, yers?' sniffed Freddie, still highly suspicious. 'What sort of work would that be, then?'

'Just about anything!' I laughed, too hearty by far. 'Painting, decorating, odd-jobs around the house. I've just put in a loft-ladder for Ang . . . for Mrs. Lambert – and for her next-door neighbour, Mrs. Pinkerton.'

'Oh, yers?' he said again, his eyes all over me. 'Must say you don't look much like a workin' lad in that gear, Shifty. Business must be bloody good already. Don't see why we should 'elp you tout for more.'

My mouth dropped open. I felt as though I'd run headlong into a brick wall. 'Well, I . . .'

'Freddie!' Millie protested laughingly. 'Don't be such an old grouch! Just because he's got one lovely suit doesn't mean he's making a fortune – you should know that.'

'Yers, well, I don't like it. I don't like the idea of *my* wife pesterin' *my* friends at *my* party – drummin' up business for a bloke we've never set eyes on before.'

'Freddie, for heaven's sake, I'm not drumming up business! All I'm doing is introducing him to a few people . . .'

'Well, Angela Lambert shouldn't have arsked you!' he retorted, beginning to move away, flinging over his shoulder, 'You're welcome to have a drink, Shifty, but this is a private party – not a bleedin' employment agency.'

And then he was gone, heading for the bar.

'Oh, God . . .' I croaked, shaking all through. 'I'd better go.'

'You'll do no such thing,' rapped Millie. 'The rude pig. He seems to forget it's my party too.'

'Millie . . . I don't want to get you into trouble.'

'Ha! I'm never out of it. I can't even ask the milkman for an extra pint without Freddie accusing me of going to bed with

145

him.' She grinned suddenly. 'Mind you, our milkman *is* kind of dishy.' She caught my arm. 'Don't mind him, Albert, he's always like this at first with the good-looking ones. But let him get used to seeing you around and he'll be slapping you on the back and telling you dirty stories.'

I grinned, not believing a word of it.

'Come on, let's get a drink,' she said brightly, adding with a wink, 'and pretend that's all you came for.'

*   *   *

The next hour was pretty miserable. Millie, deciding tact would be more profitable than defiance, bid me a temporary adieu and left me to my own devices.

Feeling Freddie's eyes on me, even when he had his back to me, I put on a forlorn stranger-lost-in-the-crowd expression and spent most of the time alone at the end of the bar furthest from Freddie, who was laughing and joking with a group of his Belview cronies.

There I stood, sipping a drink, ostensibly watching the dancers but in fact keeping an eye on Freddie and trying to decide whether I should brazen it out or cut my losses and run.

It would be a terrible pity if I had to run, I thought, because there was now no doubt that a fortune awaited me through the influential Millie. She was obviously sold on the idea of making Albert rich – as much, I suspected, to spite her husband as anything else – and it would be a crying shame to chuck away such a golden opportunity for the sake of a little nerve.

Granted, commonsense told me, I already *had* a good thing going – through Liz, Rita and their contacts – without risking life and limb, but Millie represented the jam and cream on top of that life-giving bread, and I was buggered if I was going to give it up just because Freddie hated my suit!

I threw him another glance, catching him looking sideways at me. I offered him a wan smile but he turned away immediately, said something to his mates – three more window-cleaner types – who burst into laughter, each in turn throwing me a glance as subtle as a knee in the balls.

I turned hot round the collar. They were mocking me, probably mocking my suit. I felt very uncomfortable and suddenly knew it was time to go home. The situation was impossible.

146

Right, I thought, well screw them. At least I'll go out staunchly. I'll walk right over there and confront the fat slob, thank him for a wonderful evening. At least it might help Millie.

I put down my glass, drew a deep breath to calm the nerves, and made my way over, arriving as the three men burst into raucous laughter at something Freddie had told them.

Freddie, sensing me at his elbow, swung round.

'Sorry to intrude,' I said, 'but I'm off. Just wanted to thank you for a great party, Mister Armstrong . . .'

His face fell. 'Orf? Already? Christ, it's only just started, lad. You can't go 'ome yet! Here, have another and meet the boys. This here's Frank Rudge . . . Billie Sharples . . . and Bernie King. This is Albert . . .'

'Shifty,' I said, shaking hands with them.

'Yeh – Shifty. What you drinkin', Albert?'

'Vodka tonic, thank you.'

' 'Ey, Jack! Vodka tonic for me mate here!'

Blimey, what a turn-about! Millie had been right!

'Albert's in business for himself,' explained Freddie. 'Paintin', decoratin', loft-ladders – that's right, mate, isn't it?'

'Er, yes . . . pretty well any job around the house.'

'Where you operate from, den?' asked Frank Rudge, a small, heavy-shouldered man with a broken nose, who looked capable of cracking coconuts with his teeth.

'Fulham. I . . .'

'Business good, is it?' enquired Billie Sharples, a weasel with sly, darting eyes.

I shrugged. 'It could be better.'

'Yuh can say that again,' gruffed Bernie King, his muscles rippling beneath his jacket as he brought a pint glass to his mouth.

A salubrious trio, I thought. I wouldn't trust any of them as far as I could throw Freddie.

'Nice bit o' whistle,' sniffed Frank Rudge, eyeing my suit.

'Yers, very flash,' grinned Bernie King.

'His business transactions must be all cash,' smirked Billie Sharples. 'Never 'eard of income tax returns, 'ave you, son? Well, join the club – we don't believe in handing over our hard-earned lolly to them bleeders, either.'

147

''ear, 'ear,' agreed Bernie King, raising a toast. 'I go along wiv them sentiments all the way.'

'Oh, our Albert's got his head screwed on the right way,' said Freddie Armstrong in congratulatory tone. 'He's even got my missus drummin' up business for him, ain't you, son?'

'Well . . . I . . .'

He burst out laughing and flung a tree-trunk arm round my shoulder. 'Nah, don't mind me, lad, I wus only taking the mick. Get it where you can, is my motto. Christ, we've all come up the hard way, *I* know what you're going through. Blimey, it was only two years ago that Freddie Armstrong was on his uppers! I admire your spirit! You get it how and where you can.'

'Well, that's . . . very kind of you, Mister Armstrong . . .'

'And cut that "Mister Armstrong" stuff out – I'm Freddie to my mates.'

'. . . Freddie. I felt very badly about upsetting you before. I really didn't think you'd mind . . .'

'Nah, forget it, forget it. I 'ad things on me mind. 'Ere – get this down you . . .' he handed me my drink. 'An' for Crissake enjoy yourself – you look as miserable as sin. Grab one of them good-lookin' birds over there and have a dance . . . have a swim . . . have somethin' to eat. Take your bleedin' tie off and relax, you'll be givin' my party a bad name!'

'Well, thanks very much,' I grinned. 'It's very kind of you.'

'Go on,' he waved, 'push orf and enjoy yourself – and no more of that goin' home rubbish, eh?'

'No, all right.'

I nodded to the three heavies and moved away, heart singing. I'd done it! He'd given me the go-ahead! Nothing could stop me now. I was on my way!

With my spirits doing an Irish jig, I made my way back to the other end of the bar, searching the crowd for Millie. I couldn't wait to tell her. She'd be delighted, too.

Ho *ho*, what a future lay ahead for me. I could feel it, taste it, see it . . . I'd get an office, a new van, more staff, then it would build and build over the months to come into something really terrific, eventually into twenty . . . maybe *fifty* vans on the road, just like Dyno-rod – with the chairman, Albert Shifty, directing operations from a fabulous office in Knightsbridge.

And the name of the firm?

Let Albert Do It!

Why not!

Yes, I could hear the girls on my switchboard answering the clammering phones. 'Good morning . . . Let Albert Do It! A loft-ladder? Certainly, madam, a van will call within the hour.'

How many houses were there in the London area alone? Three million? Something like that. Three million loft-ladders at a hundred and twenty five quid each . . .

I ran cold at the thought. It was . . . three hundred and seventy five *million* quid! No, it couldn't be, I must have stuck on too many noughts . . .

'What are you doing?' murmured a voice behind me. 'Making out your last will and testament?'

It was Millie!

'Don't turn round – he's watching!' she hissed.

I did turn round, grinning at her. 'It's all right! I've had a word with him! It was just like you said – he threw his arm round me and called me mate!'

She deflated with relief. 'Thank God. What did he say exactly?'

'That he admired my push . . . that he didn't blame me for getting business where I could . . . that he'd started off the same way.'

'That's true. Well, well, well . . .' she grinned, 'the mind positively *swims* at the possibilities.'

She was *not*, I felt, referring solely to *my* future welfare.

'Yes,' I smiled, 'doesn't it.'

'Mmm . . .' she mused, subduing a delighted smile. 'In that case, we shall revert to our previous plan. Let's just . . . take things *nice* and easy, Albert, and at the appropriate moment . . .' She raised her glass, her eyes incinerating me over the rim. 'He'll be going to bed soon.'

'He will?'

'He starts work *very* early.'

'How commendable. Won't you be going, too?'

She replied with a husky laugh and made to move away. 'I'll be seeing you, Albert.'

'Toodle-oo, Mrs. A.'

CHAPTER THIRTEEN

The signal came about half-past one.

The party was going full-throttle, everyone well-juiced and making a terrific din, mostly round the pool now in which a couple of dozen guests were having great fun trying to drown each other.

There was no sign of Freddie, nor had there been for quite a while. The last time I'd seen him he'd looked extremely stewed and I reckoned he'd gone to bed as Millie had said.

I was standing in the shadow of the diving tower, watching the antics in the pool and thinking about Millie, wondering where she'd got to, when suddenly, from behind me, came a 'Psssst!'

I turned, peered into the bushes, and saw her, beckoning me over. With a final check that nobody was watching, I backed up, then turned and slipped into the bushes.

'Quickly!' she whispered, taking my hand.

Beyond this protective line of bushes we broke out into a wide stretch of moonlit lawn. Here she veered off to the right and used the deep shadow of a high hedge to cover our progress down the lawn. At the far end we entered a dense thicket of bushes, but with great sureness she guided me through, until eventually we emerged into a little glade lit brightly by the full moon.

And there, in front of us, stood the summerhouse – a large, wooden, Swiss-chalet type of building with steps leading up to a verandah.

'My retreat from insanity,' she announced, leading me up the steps and through the door.

She touched a light-switch and brought the room to life. It was a cozy, colourful room with cane furniture and a stone fireplace. Over on the left stood the bar, and in an alcove on the right – the water bed.

Millie crossed to the bar, doing a pirouette in the centre of the floor to embrace the room. 'Do you like it?'

She was *very* tiddly.

'I think it's fabulous,' I said, following her over. 'Do you spend a lot of time here, Millie?'

Behind the bar, she set up glasses, answering me as she poured two enormous gins. 'Hours and hours . . . dreaming mostly.'

'Of what?'

She smiled. 'Knights in shining armour.'

She handed me my drink, raised hers in a tipsy toast. 'To knights in shining armour.' She drank some and put down her glass, reached under the bar and clicked a switch. 'Let's have some appropriate music . . .'

As soft, romantic strings filled the room, she came round the bar and slipped her arms round my neck, eased her body hard into mine and snuggled into my ear, moaning softly, 'Oh, that's beautiful . . . so-o-o beautiful.' She sighed contentedly. 'Albert . . . ?'

'Yes, Millie?'

'Will you be my knight in shining armour?'

'Yes, Millie . . . though I'll have to be careful of my spurs in your water bed.'

She threw back her head and shrieked with laughter, then kissed me on the nose. 'Oh, I like you, you make me laugh. Always make me laugh, Albert.'

'I'll do my best.'

'That's how it must be, Albert. If you ever get serious I shall tickle you till you stop. Are you ticklish, Albert? Hmmm? . . . Hmmm . . . ?'

She drove fingers into my ribs, buckling my knees. 'Millie, stop that! Stop it . . . !'

'Ha ha! I've found your ticklish spot! Ooooh . . . ahhh . . . eeeeh . . . !'

'Millie . . . STOP . . . !'

'And how many other ticklish spots have you got, Albert . . . hmmm? . . . ehh?'

Her hands were all over me, probing there, prodding here, driving me backwards towards the bed. Now it was right behind me. I fell backwards . . . and bounced . . . boing, boing!

'Hey!' I exclaimed. 'This is terrific!'

'Didn't I tell you!' she laughed, and took a flyer onto the bed, bouncing on it like a trampoline. 'Wheeee . . . !

Wheee . . . ! And just . . . imagine . . . what it's like . . . making *love* on it!'

She suddenly came to rest, panting, and looked at me, her eyes excited, wildly alive. '*Can* you imagine what it's like, Albert?'

I nodded, grinning. 'I reckon.'

She rolled towards me and kissed me, hard, finally breaking away with a gasp. 'Oh, boy . . .' and turning on to her back. Her hands moved to the buttons on her dress. 'Albert . . .'

'Yes, Millie?'

'Get out of that *beauti*ful suit.'

'Yes, Millie.'

I slid off the bed and got a hand to the button on my jacket – and that was all I got. In the next instant the door exploded open – and there stood Freddie! . . . eyes glowing maniacally, fingers flexing, aching to get at me.

'You BAS . . . TAAAARD!' he bellowed, shaking the room. 'I'LL FUCKING *KILL* YOU!'

And in he galloped.

Millie's scream rent the night. 'FREDDIE . . . NO!'

'NnnnnnnYYAAAAAAHHHHHH!' he roared, making a wild grab for me. I ducked, ran under his arm . . . but he managed to grab a pocket.

RiiiIIIIIPPPP! Away it came, taking a square foot of jacket with it.

'DaaaaAAAAAAHHHHH!' he bellowed, making another murderous grab.

I leapt behind the bar, dodged, feinted, wrong-footed him and was away across the room, heading for the door. I'd made it! I was out of the door! I was free . . . !

CRUUUMMMPPP!!

Straight into the waiting arms of Big Boy Bernie King.

'Gotcha!' he chuckled.

Frank Rudge leapt out of a bush. 'We got 'im, Freddie!' he shouted, then went for my ankles and lifted me horizontally.

'We certainly have,' wheedled Billie Sharples, jumping in for a throttling head-lock.

Out thundered Freddie, twenty-two stone of ungovernable fury, and brandished under my nose a fist as big as a boulder. 'I'm gonna fix you *good*, pretty boy!' he seethed, froth forming at the corners of his mouth. 'I'm gonna make sure that my missus is the last bird *you'll* ever rumble, sunshine – 'cause by the time I finish wiv you, you won't have enough cock left to fill a thimble! Right, lads – take him to the cellars!'

Christ, they were going to do it! They were going to amputate me old mate! They wouldn't! They couldn't!

They bloody could!

Into the woods they plunged, carrying me like a battering-ram, face down, the dark earth rushing beneath me at terrible speed. I felt sick, dizzy. I wanted to cry out, shout, protest, plead, beg, wheedle, promise . . . but nothing but blank disbelief came out. This could not be happening to me!

Well, serves you damn-well right, Shifty, you should have stayed in your own backyard. This is what comes from social climbing! You don't belong here – you *belong* in Chez Kranki with the smells and the terrible cooking and the crumby guests and randy little Fritz . . .

Oh, yes, yes . . . please God let it be a dream . . . let me wake up in my room in Buchenwald right now . . . *please!* Do this one thing for me and I'll never ask for anything else again – *ever!*

Get lost, said God, this is judgement day, Shifty. This is where you get yours for screwing around with married women, for taking liberties, being too damn cocky, too ambitious, too big for your boots. Torment time is coming up fast – in about three minutes from now!

Wooomf! Suddenly it was light! We were out of the woods and jogging across the lawn, heading for the pool.

At the risk of snapping my neck I looked up . . . saw the pool was totally deserted, not a soul in sight to save me!

'Okay, lads, get him up!' commanded Freddie.

They veered towards the diving tower, burly Bernie King in the lead, bearing the weight of my shoulders, the others behind, carrying my legs.

We reached the tower and up King went one-handed, the others shoving and pushing me up the ladder . . . up and up and up. Bang, thump, thud . . . every bit of me hit that ladder as I was hauled to the top.

Then I was there . . . twenty feet above the turquoise pool, once again horizontal, staring down at that appalling drop.

'Just a little somethin' to cool your blood before we spill it!' snarled Freddie. 'Okay, lads, let the bastard have it!'

'A-one . . . a-two . . . and a-THREEEE . . . !'

Out I shot like a bleeding torpedo, then I crumpled, splayed out like a star-fish, and in a whirl of flying arms and legs catherine-wheeled down to land with an almighty crack on my back in the water.

WHOOOFFF! the air exploded from my lungs. Down I sank, the world about me a confusion of lights and bubbles. Then I hit bottom and up I shot, breaking surface in dire panic, arms flailing, lungs bursting, racked by coughing, my mind seized by one desperate thought – to get away from those homicidal maniacs!

Get to the side before they have a chance to get down the tower! Get out and run! Swim . . . swim . . . like you've never swum before!

I thrashed out like a madman, the weight of water in my clothes dragging me back, pulling me down . . . down. I'd never make it! I was going to drown! No, I wasn't! The side of the pool was within my reach! I lunged . . . caught hold of the edge . . . got my other hand to it and hauled myself up . . . and came face-to-face with FREDDIE!

'YAAAHHHH . . . !' I yelled.

'Now, lissen to me, pretty boy . . .' he said reasonably, with the quiet calm of a poised cobra. 'The only thing that's saved you from losing your meat an' two veg is that I know you didn't have it orf wiv my missus. If you *had*, me old love, they'd have found your dickless remains on Wimbledon Common tomorrow mornin' – see. So thank your lucky stars you didn't get it up. *But*, me old charmer, if you so much as set foot in this vicinity again . . . *or* in the vicinity of my old stompin' ground – Belview Estate – me and my mates are goin' to hang you up in my cellar, place your knackers in an iron vice, and tighten it till they pop! Get the message?'

'Gulp,' I glugged.

'*Then* . . . we shall tie big weights to your old man and stretch him till he looks like a yard and a half of clothes-line . . . and *then* we shall sever said clothes-line with a pair of garden shears. Get *that* message?'

'Glug,' I gulped.

'All right, me old son, now ... GET THE FUCK OFF MY PROPERTY!!'

POW!

And just for good measure he punched me on the nose.

CHAPTER FOURTEEN

No sorrier sight in all this world has anyone seen than the one that dragged itself out of the van and up the steps to the front door of Chez Kranki.

Soaked to the skin, my beautiful whistle torn, crumpled, spattered with blood from my throbbing conk, green dye from my tie staining my primrose yellow shirt, one shoe lost . . . I looked as though I'd been put through a nine-hour car-wash and bloody-well felt like it.

Easing open the front door, I popped my head in, made sure the coast was clear, then crept in and across the hall. And with one foot on the stairs, Fritz came hurtling out of the shadows.

'Aw, no . . .' I groaned, then gave up and stuck my right leg out, too exhausted and dispirited to offer resistance. 'Go on, mate, have a go. Personally I'm giving it up for ever, gets you in nothing but trouble.'

I waited . . . but nothing was happening! I looked down. Blimey, he was skulking away! He didn't fancy me any more! Well, rotten hell . . .

I started up the stairs, consumed with depression, finally reached the top and collapsed.

Norman's door jerked open. 'Alb . . . bloody hell, what happened to you!'

I raised my head and grinned pitifully. '*Boy*, what a party . . . you should have been there. I collected this lot in the Paul Jones! The birds went *mad* for me. Eighteen of them fighting like wild-cats to get me.'

'Gerraway!' he gasped.

I crawled into my room on my hands and knees, staggered to my feet and collapsed across the bed. 'Norman . . .' I groaned, 'I have well and truly screwed us up, son. I reached for the stars and grabbed a big fat handful of nothing. Really thought we had it made tonight . . . money galore. And we had, too, but for one small mistake . . .'

'Oh?' he said quietly, mystified. 'What was that, Albert?'

'I picked the wrong bleeding husband. Fat Freddie Armstrong – King of Belview Estate. We're finished there, old friend. From tonight it's out of bounds – under penalty of something worse than death.'

'What's worse than death, Albert?'

'Having your cock cut off.'

'Eh!'

'I kid you not, that's what he promised.'

'Ooooh,' he winced.

'Finished,' I sighed despairingly. 'Six hundred potential loft-ladders up the shoot, Norman – I've lost us a fortune. Well, it's taught me a lesson, I can tell you. No more lonely married women on suburban housing estates for me. From now on it's going to be strictly business – a blocked lavatory here, a filthy oven there . . .'

'Oh . . .'

The poor lad sounded broken hearted.

'Do you really mean that, Albert?'

'Every word of it, Norman. I cannot . . . *will* not . . . expose you to the danger that I myself . . .'

'I mean – about loft-ladders . . . and housing estates.'

I turned my head and looked at him, puzzled by his tone, his persistence. 'Well, yes . . . why?'

'Oh, that's a blow,' he muttered miserably. 'Because . . . well, I had a nice surprise for you . . .'

I raised my head, a small fluttering of hope quickening my heart. 'What . . . sort of surprise, Norman?'

He grinned sheepishly. 'Well . . . bein' here by meself tonight and fed up with the room, I took a bus ride to Merton Park. And on the way I passed . . . a big new housing estate, just off the by-pass. Oooh, I thought, what's good for Belview might be good for this one, so I . . . I got off the bus and took a walk into the estate.'

I sat up, staring at him, amazed at this revelation of business acumen. 'You crafty basket . . . go on.'

'Well, I was walkin' along one of the streets – there's dozens of them, Albert . . . must be a thousand houses there! It's *enormous*! . . . and suddenly I spot this bird weeding her front garden, nice lookin' she was, wearin' a pair of shorts, smashing legs and . . . and anyway, as I pass her, she gives me a smile and asks if I've got a light for her fag. So I give her one and she starts talkin' to me, asks me if I live on the estate and I say no and she says . . .'

'Norman! Cut out the drivel – what was the outcome!'

He grinned angelically. 'I flogged her a loft-ladder.'

I gaped at him. 'You . . .'

'I did! Straight up! I gave her one of your cards and . . . we got the job for Monday!'

I leapt off the bed and embraced him. 'Norman, you . . . mmmmuuuhh!' I kissed him on top of the head.

'Aw, eh, Albert . . .' he grinned. 'It was only a blinkin' loft-ladder.'

I backed away, shaking my head. 'No, Norman, no! Not just *one* loft-ladder . . . perhaps a *thousand* loft-ladders! Think of it – one thousand loft-ladders at one hundred and twenty five pounds each! That's . . . I'll work it out tomorrow.'

'There's . . . only one drawback, though, Albert . . .' he said dolefully.

My heart sank as disaster once again loomed. 'Oh? And what's that, Norman?'

'She's married,' he said, grinning ear-to-ear. 'To a sailor . . . who's bin at sea for almost a year.'

Oh, suffering mother . . . here we go again.

Keep an eye on the obituary columns for further news of Albert Shifty.

Bye for now.

'A whole *year*, Norman . . . ?'

'Straight up,' he nodded. 'And what's more, she's just had a telegram to say he won't be home for *another* three months! I felt really sorry for her . . . she sounded ever so lonely . . . said she'd look forward to Monday for a bit of company . . .'

HUMOUR

0426		Tandem	
	158350	Tony Blackburn **A LAUGH IN EVERY POCKET**	40p
	075870	Hugh Burnett 'Those Marvellous Monks!' (cartoons) **BEWARE OF THE ABBOT**	25p
	075951	**BOOK OF THE MONK**	25p
	07579X	**NOTHING SACRED**	25p
	075609	**SACRED & CONFIDENTIAL**	25p
	076087	**TOP SACRED**	25p
	136616	**DARLING — YOU ARE A DEVIL!**	50p*
	076249	Lynda Mallet **ALL BRA YESTERDAYS**	50p*
	07632X	**MALLET'S BRA BOOK**	50p*
	139607	Spike Milligan **THE BEDSIDE MILLIGAN**	30p
	139879	**A BOOK OF BITS OR A BIT OF A BOOK**	30p
	139526	**A DUSTBIN OF MILLIGAN**	30p
	139798	**THE LITTLE POT BOILER**	30p
	165470	**SEXY CROSSWORDS**	50p*
	157559	Hugh de Witt **BAWDY BARRACK-ROOM BALLADS**	35p

*Not for sale in Canada

Wyndham Books are available from many booksellers and newsagents. If you have any difficulty please send purchase price plus postage on the scale below to:

Wyndham Cash Sales,   or Star Book Service,
123 King Street,   GPO Box 29,
London W6 9JG   Isle of Man,
                       British Isles

Whilst every effort is made to keep prices low, it is sometimes necessary to increase prices at short notice. Wyndham Books reserve the right to show new retail prices on covers which may differ from those advertised in the text or elsewhere.

UK AND EIRE
One book: 15p plus 7p per copy for each additional book ordered to a maximum charge of 57p.

OTHER COUNTRIES
Rates available on request.

NB These charges are subject to Post Office charge fluctuations.